What does a man do, when his wagon trains have been attacked, set fire to, his cotton bales burnt up, his mules out of their minds with terror and pain?

He finds a way to get more wagons, and mules, and cotton.

He keeps his freighting going.

What does a man do when he is captured and tortured to make him stop hauling cotton?

He finds a way to escape. He kills whichever of his torturers he can find—

And he keeps the freighters running.

What happens when he is betrayed by his friend? What if he has to kill the man who is brother to the woman he wants to marry?

He finds out that there are things in war that are a helluva lot tougher than fighting it.

ELMER KELTON

BITTER TRAIL

A TOM DOHERTY ASSOCIATES BOOK
NEW YORK

This is a work of fiction. All the characters and events portrayed in this book are either products of the author's imagination or are used fictitiously.

BITTER TRAIL

Cover art by Darell K. Sweet

A Forge Book
Published by Tom Doherty Associates, Inc.
175 Fifth Avenue
New York, NY 10010

Forge® is a registered trademark of Tom Doherty Associates, Inc.

ISBN: 0-812-55118-4

First Forge edition: June 1996

Printed in the United States of America

0 9 8 7 6 5 4 3 2 1

1

THE HORSE TRACKS APPEARED suddenly out of the chaparral, milled in brief disorder, then struck northward up the crooked wagon trail that snaked its dusty way through the mesquite and catclaw and prickly pear.

Coming upon the tracks, Frio Wheeler reined his horse to a quick stop. His hand dropped instinctively toward the stock of the saddlegun beneath his leg. He peered through narrowed eyes at the trail, which disappeared into the rippling late-summer heatwaves and hostile brush. He took off his flat-brimmed black hat to wipe dust-thickened perspiration onto his sleeve and turned to the Mexican who rode beside him.

"What do you make of it, Blas?"

Sombreroed Blas Talamantes turned in his big-horned Mexico saddle to look at the tracks as they led out of the mesquite. Sweat-soaked, his homemade cotton shirt clung to his back.

"Twelve, maybeso fifteen horses."

Frio Wheeler stepped from the saddle and squatted on the ground for a close look. He fingered the tracks. Not very old—an hour or two, maybe. Made since daylight, at least. "A few years ago, I'd've said Indians."

Blas Talamantes shook his head and pointed. "A piece of cigar, Frio, over there. Vaqueros, maybe?"

"Maybe cowboys. More likely renegades from across the Rio." Wheeler swung back onto his horse, took a grim look across the drought-stricken country, and brought the saddlegun up into his lap. "Best listen hard, Blas, and keep our eyes peeled. There's a war on."

This was the Rio Grande country of Texas in 1863, a small extension of the bloody conflict ablaze upon the battlefields of Virginia and Tennessee, upon the green rolling hills of Gettysburg. Here on the underbelly of the Confederacy lay the South's only open border, its only port free of the Union blockade. Along this thorn-studded trail to the Rio Grande, dust boiled high over trains of mule-drawn wagons and ox-drawn carts, carrying their heavy burden of Confederate cotton southward to be sold across the river in Mexico. Moving north, the same trains would carry war supplies for the Trans-Mississippi Department of the Confederacy—rifles, powder and bar lead, sulphur, mercury, and cloth.

At the end of this trail across the barren sands and the forbidding chaparral waited the twin cities of the Rio—Brownsville on the Texas bank, Matamoros on the Mexican. Once sleepy border towns, separated by the sluggish waters of the muddy Bravo, they had awakened to the rattle of sabers and the boom of cannon. They were swollen now and bustling with the international commerce of war. Gold coin clinked to the groan of wagon wheels, and tequila spilled in the streets.

Though this was a long way from Virginia, men rode with eyes open and their guns ready to use, for the hatreds of war had come to the Rio. By the hundreds, Texans with Union sympathies had fled southward across the river. Some had gone north by boat from Bagdad and other Mexican ports to join Lincoln's forces and wear the blue. Others remained in Mexico. Many of these waited impatiently in Matamoros, listening eagerly for war news, looking across the river with longing eyes at a homeland that now had become an enemy. Sometimes, in league with border bandits of either Anglo or Mexican blood, these men swam the river at night to raid and burn in the name of the Union, then ride back to sanctuary across that narrow, muddy boundary. *Renegados*, the Confederate Texans called them, using the Mexican name. It was a time of indistinct loyalties and confused hatreds, when friends had become enemies and old enemies had somehow become friends—a mixed-up time when all the rules had been lost. . . .

Frio Wheeler touched big-roweled Mexican spurs to his sorrel's ribs and moved him into an easy trot. Wheeler sat upright in the saddle, shoulders squared with a pride born of his place and time. He was in his early thirties, though it would have been hard to guess his age from looking at him. He was a man seldom under roof. His skin was burned Mexican-brown from the scorching sun of Texas's ancient Camino Real, the Royal Road, and from wagon trails through the Wild Horse Desert and the chaparral. His brown hair, which needed a cutting, was beginning to show a glint of gray. Turkey tracks had bitten deep at the corners of his blue eyes, for he habitually squinted against the glare of the sun-drenched land.

Riding beside him, Blas Talamantes was the more spectacular. His high-peaked Mexican sombrero was twice as wide as Wheeler's plain old black hat. His brown leather breeches were decorated with lacing laboriously sewn by a loving woman's nimble fingers. Wheeler had allowed his big spurs to darken with grime and tarnish, but Talamantes had kept his own polished to a bright silver. Both men rode with collars and sleeves buttoned against the sun.

There was much about them that was similar—size, build, and age. By a like token there was much that was different—their upbringing, their heritage of two cultures a world apart. To Wheeler, the first consideration always was to tend to the business at hand. To Blas, business was not unimportant, but a man should also seek out whatever beauty, love, and adventure the day might yield, for there might not be a tomorrow; and if there were no tomorrow, the business would have been of little import.

The two men had ridden together a long time now, and the things about them that were different had been put aside. Wheeler was *patrón*, and Talamantes was the man hired. But over and beyond that, they were *compadres*, so that it was not always apparent who was *patrón* and who was *empleado*.

Blas Talamantes had the better ears. "Frio, I hear shooting."

Frio stopped and slowly turned his head, seeking the sound. It came to him on the hot breeze from uptrail.

"*Renegados*," he guessed, his mouth drawn tight. "They've hit some small outfit that's short of men."

"Maybe yours," said Blas.

They rode on with their rifles ready. The firing was nearer now, dropping down to a few sporadic shots and eventually stopping altogether. Presently they saw white smoke begin to spiral upward over the brush.

"Cotton smoke," Frio said. "I expect that's some CSA bales that'll never make it to Matamoros."

They heard hoofbeats drumming toward them. Frio jerked his head to one side, signaling Blas to pull out of the trail. "Two of us couldn't dent them much," he said, "but they could plow us under."

This was a hostile country where almost everything went armed for its own protection, whether it be plant life or animal. The thick mesquites and catclaws at trailside were white-flecked with cotton scraps that their tough thorns had ripped from bale-laden wagons. Frio and Blas sought a way through this brush and the thick growth of man-tall prickly pear. They dismounted, rifles in hand, and stood with fingers over their horses' nostrils. The sound of the hooves came louder, and Frio could glimpse a flash of movement.

Watching over a tall clump of pear, he saw the men pass by in a jog trot. He saw the black-clad Mexican in front, wearing a sombrero so wide that in the afternoon sun it cast a shadow to his waist. He saw the two Anglos who moved side by side, half a length behind the Mexican. Trailing these, a dozen more riders straggled along, all of them apparently Mexican. They led four strings of mules, these still wearing the harness with which they had drawn the cotton wagons. Trace chains rattled from the steady swing of their pace.

The men passed, but the gray dust still hovered a while behind them, drifting at last out into the heavy brush.

Frio Wheeler's eyes glowed with helpless anger.

"My mules." He swung back into the saddle, Blas following suit. "Blas, did you see who was ridin' out in front?"

Blas nodded, his mouth grim. "Florencio Chapa! *Bandido muy malo*, with a heart like a grinder's stone." He paused, looking at the ground. "The gringos, you see who they are?"

Gringo could be a fighting word on the border if used in the wrong tone. But there was no offense in the matter-of-fact way Blas said it.

Frio's jaw ridged with regret for what he had seen. He knew from Blas's eyes that the Mexican had known the men. "You mean Tom McCasland? Yes, I recognized him."

"He is your best friend, Frio. Or he *was*." The last came more like a question.

"War changes things, Blas."

"That other gringo, he is Bige Campsey. In the old days Tom McCasland would never ride with a man like Campsey."

Frio shook his head. "Like I said, war makes a man do lots of things. Come on, we best go see how bad the damage is."

They found five wagons strung out in the trail. The one in the lead, loaded with burning cotton bales, collapsed in a shower of sparks as Frio and Blas rode up. The other four wagons were being saved, though the Mexican teamsters were letting themselves be scorched to push burning bales out of the wagon beds and onto the ground. Without asking questions, Frio and Blas pitched in to help. They tossed their rawhide ropes over the tops of smoldering bales and spurred their horses out, dallying the ropes around their saddlehorns and pulling the bales down from the wagons.

The raiders had missed dumping some of the water

barrels. A sandy-haired young Texan was running back and forth, dipping water and pitching it onto a wagon, dousing flames. With the bales out of the way, some of the Mexican freighting crew shoveled dirt over the fires, slowly snúffing them out.

Cotton smoke is a hard kind to take, and the choking smell of it clung awhile from the still-smouldering bales that lay about in scattered confusion. Cotton-bale fires were difficult to kill, but Frio thought most of these were under control. He had already given up on the sixteen bales in the collapsed lead wagon. A few others also were too far gone to save, for the stubborn fires would continue to eat away like cancer within the heart of the bales.

Without taking time for a close look, Frio decided four of the five wagons could be salvaged. Damage appeared to range from slight to rather bad, but none beyond repair. They were the big prairie-schooner kind of freight wagons with twenty-four-foot bed, the hind wheels almost six feet tall, the front ones just short of five—solid-iron axles, the wagon tires six inches wide and an inch thick. Hell-and-high-water wagons, these were. In this dry country they saw mostly hell.

A Mexican teamster came leading ten mules out of an opening in the brush. The only team that had been saved, they still wore their harness. The mules danced wild-eyed, smelling the smoke. But the teamster was talking to them in fast-flowing Spanish that included some profanity, and they weren't going to give him much trouble.

Frio wiped grimy sweat onto his sleeve. He looked around for the sandy-haired boy. "What about it, Happy? Anybody hurt?"

Happy Jack Fleet had only recently come of age,

and the excitement of the skirmish still played in his eyes. There was, indeed, a happy look on his smoke-smudged face. That the kid had actually enjoyed this fight came as a surprise to Frio, though on reflection he knew it shouldn't. From the beginning, Happy had struck Frio as the kind who would charge a bear with a slingshot and laugh as he did it. He wasn't old enough to have had the wildness stomped out of him.

Happy said, "They hit one man in the shoulder. Antonio Garza, on the lead wagon. Nobody killed."

Frio nodded, glad it hadn't been worse. "Guess it's foolish to ask what happened."

"They came on us all of a sudden." Happy's voice still carried a remnant of the fight's intoxication. "Wasn't time for us to circle up, even if there'd been room to." He glanced at the pear and thorny brush that closed in tight alongside the trail. "All we could do was pile off and take to the pear. They had things pretty much to suit theirselves, except that we kept them dodgin' some. They set fire to the cotton and cut loose the teams, all but the last one. We had it too well covered."

Frio said, "I expect you did the best you could."

Happy's eyes laughed a little. "Them Mexicans of yours are teamsters, not soldiers. They couldn't hit the side of a barn if they was locked up in it."

"I hired them to skin mules. Didn't figure on them havin' to fight."

"You may need to figure on it from now on."

They walked over to where the wounded man had been stretched out on the ground, a dirty blanket under him. The head teamster, known as the *caporal*, was trying to slow the blood and get a look at the bullet hole. In Spanish he said, "Flaco, build a fire. We have to take the bullet out."

The wounded man groaned his dread, but he made no further protest. The Mexican people had a way of shrugging their shoulders and taking whatever misfortune fate chose to hand them, and there was usually enough of it to go around. The fire was built and the water put on to boil. When all was ready, the *caporal* turned to Frio.

"*Patrón,* you have the steadiest hands of any man I know. Will you do what has to be done?"

They had brought up all the tequila that was left on the train. It wasn't much, for the trip to Brownsville was nearly over. But the wounded man was so drunk by the time the operation began that he had little idea what was happening. He fainted shortly, and the job went with ease from there on. Done, Frio let the wound bleed a little to wash it clean and turned the rest of the task over to the *caporal.*

Happy Jack had watched without a comment. Now he turned away with Frio. "They're a hardy breed, these Mexicans. You can't kill one of them with a double-bitted ax. Small wonder there's so many of them."

To the people who were acquainted with him around here, the kid was simply Happy Jack, a cowboy and nothing more. He had come riding down one day from what in that time was known as West Texas—a little way beyond San Antonio. He bore a cowboy's quiet distrust of anyone who didn't ride a horse. With the rash pride of youth he felt he was a man sufficient unto himself.

"I guess you got a look at your ranch," he said to Frio.

Frio nodded. He had started these five loaded wagons south from San Antonio, then had left them in the rolling live-oak hills. He had ridden ahead at a fast pace to have time for a quick look over his ranch and still catch the wagons before they completed the more than two hundred miles to Brownsville and Matamoros.

Frio Wheeler had drifted down to this region several years ago from his home territory along the Frio River. He had found there was room here; room for a man to grow big if he started early enough and helped push an undeveloped land. Captain Richard King was doing it on his ranch along Santa Gertrudis Creek. Frio had seen no reason he couldn't do likewise in the brush-land and the coastal prairies of the lower Rio Grande. He had brought cattle here and started to build. It had looked as if the future was unlimited. Then had come the war.

It wasn't that the South didn't need beef; it did, and desperately. But distance was one of the enemies here. It was one thing to haul cotton and other nonperishables overland a thousand miles and more. It was quite another to drive cattle. It had been tried and abandoned as an impractical job. South Texas cattle had slumped in value. Frio Wheeler had raised a stake and gone to freighting, for this way he could mark time and hang onto his part of the ranch while doing a job that might help bring a Confederate victory. It was a job fully as important as marching off to Virginia with a rifle over his shoulder. The war wouldn't last forever. The Yankees would soon realize they couldn't whip the South, and they would come to terms both sides could live with. Then maybe a man could go back to the business of growing, of sweating a civilization out of this region the early Mexicans had called the Desert of the Dead.

Frio managed to see the ranch only occasionally anymore, but Blas Talamantes had stayed there as his *caporal.* War had drawn away most of the manpower, and they were short-handed. But Blas at least was able to hold Frio's ranch together. He was getting most of the calves branded, something many ranchers weren't able to do. The herd was steadily building because there was so little market, so few sold. When this war was over there would be old steers in that brush with horns longer than a man's arm. Perhaps then, Frio thought, a hungry North might be in the market for beef. No matter what a man thought of Yankees in general, their money spent good.

Now Happy Jack stared regretfully at the burned-up cotton bales and the ruined wagon. "I wish we could have done more, Frio."

It hurt, but Frio had picked up from the Mexican people some of their ability to shrug and turn their backs upon misfortune. "It's spilt milk now. What worries me is gettin' the rest of this cotton to the river with just one team. We'll have to load one wagon and haul it in. We'll cache the other wagons and the rest of the cotton bales in the brush till I can get fresh teams back up here. I'll leave you here in charge, Happy."

Disappointment came to Happy's eyes. "You goin' across the river to Matamoros?"

Frio nodded. "I generally do."

"That's where you'll find the ones that done this. Them two gringos that was sidin' the bandits, I expect they've got a Union flag over their door. I'd like to go help you hunt them."

Frio shook his head. "Happy, they're fair game on this side of the river. Over there, they can't touch us and we can't touch them. We can't afford to get Mexico turned against us."

"Mexico ain't goin' to turn against us. She's makin' too much money out of the cotton trade."

"Happy, last year a Unionist by the name of Montgomery joined with some Matamoros bandits on a raid in Zapata County. They killed Isidro Vela, the chief justice. He was well thought of on this side of the river. Some time later a bunch of our boys crossed over the Rio at Bagdad, caught Montgomery, and hung him. Nobody denied that he had earned it, but it almost caused Mexico to close the border. Bad as he needed killin', it wasn't worth the cost.

"Sure, it hurts to stand on the riverbank and watch somebody like that runnin' around loose on the other side. But it works as much in our favor as it does theirs. More, maybe. The Yankees keep all our ports bottled up, but there's nothin' they can do about the trade that goes out of a Mexican port. Long as Mexico stays neutral, we all win. She ever changes, we lose."

Happy Jack pursed his lips. "Then you don't aim to start no fight with them?"

"No fight."

The young man pushed his hat back and leaned against a wagon wheel, disappointed. "I reckon I'll stay here. I won't be missin' nothin'."

2

THROUGH THE AGES, THE Rio Grande had been as unpredictable as a woman. She had changed her mind dozens of times, altering her course and leaving deserted a multitude of old riverbeds that the Mexicans called *resacas*. Most of these had haired over with grass and weeds, though the drought of recent months had burned away much of the vegetation. Along the edges of some *resacas* stood the stately old palm trees that had caught the fancy of the first exploring Spaniards and had prompted them to name this the River of the Palms.

The Gulf breeze blew in welcome from the east, waving the palms and easing the heat that Frio Wheeler had borne across the sands and the heavy brush. It always pleased him to reach the first of these ancient riverbeds, for it meant Brownsville was close at hand. He and Blas Talamantes rode horseback several lengths ahead of the lone wagon with its load of smoke-blackened cotton. They passed near the old Resaca de la Palma battlefield where General Zachary Taylor and his troops had drawn some of the first blood in the Mexican War of 1846, just seventeen years ago. Lots of men who lived in Brownsville, and far more who lived across in Matamoros, had vivid memories of that fight. Frio had listened to many a bloody tale.

Far across the river stood the twin spires of the tall brick cathedral on the Mexican side. There was nothing so spectacular on the Texas bank. Brownsville was much newer than its Spanish-speaking sister, and somewhat smaller. There had been no town on this side when Taylor's troops had built the eight hundred yards of earthwork that was to become known as Fort Brown. Today Brownsville with its stone and lumber buildings still had a new look about it.

Town dogs came running out to meet and greet the riders, yapping at the heels of the horses and backing away only when Blas took down his rawhide rope. The dogs fell to one side and picked up the mules as the wagon drew close. The mules gave them less attention then they would give a mosquito.

"Blas," said Frio, "I'm goin' to lope on ahead and visit some folks. I'll see you directly down at the cottonyard."

Blas smiled thinly. "No hurry, we get there just fine." He paused, then added, "Someday maybe you better marry that girl."

Frio grinned and moved into an easy lope. He rubbed his face and found it still smooth, for he had shaved in camp that morning.

Brownsville was growing rapidly because of the war trade. Every time he came in from a trip, it seemed the town had edged a little farther out along the wagon road. People were coming in faster than houses could be built. Here and there he could see tents and Mexican-style *jacales*, thatched with reeds and broomcorn. Soon he was riding in the heart of the town, past the Miller Hotel, the new city market, the palebrick Stillman home, which had been the first permanent house in Brownsville. In the dirt streets he passed Confederate soldiers from the fort, whiling away off-duty time by making the rounds of the saloons. Mexican *dulce* vendors were attempting to sell them candies made of brown *piloncillo* sugar. The soldiers were not interested in candy, but they were plainly interested in a couple of the flashing-eyed girls who were trying to sell it.

Down beyond the brick quartermaster's fence that stood between Fort Brown and the town, General Hamilton Bee wouldn't be thinking about girls. He would be nervously studying his dispatches, wondering when and if the Yankees might land troops at the Boca Chica and march the thirty miles inland across the sea meadows to capture Brownsville. Frio could well understand why Bee would be nervous, sitting here with just four companies of the Thirty-Third Texas Cavalry, a battery of light artillery and a scattered few militia companies that he didn't altogether trust, dispersed up and down the river for three hundred miles.

With this invaluable border cotton trade and thousands of pounds of war goods coming over each day at Brownsville, it was incomprehensible to Frio that the Confederate government would let it be jeopardized by lack of troops. But one of the biggest disappointments the Southern people had suffered was the slow realization that their new government in Richmond could blunder along as foolishly as the Washington government ever did. Sometimes he thought it would be a wonder if both sides didn't lose the war.

Meade McCasland's frame mercantile store fronted on Elizabeth Street, which the pioneer merchant Charles Stillman had named for his wife. The store had a tall false front with a dummy balcony that opened from nowhere and led the same way. Gray-haired Meade McCasland never had liked that feature, for to him it smacked of deception, and there was not an ounce of deception in his soul. From the day he had bought it, he had intended to cut the storefront down to size. But these were busy times, and he had more to worry about than an unwanted balcony.

Frio Wheeler reined through the wagon traffic toward the hitchrack in front of the store. He held up, to let a droopy-mustached old Mexican pass with a burro-drawn cart and forty gallons of muddy Rio water that he would sell for two dollars a load.

A little Mexican boy of about six came bouncing off the porch, running excitedly. "Mister Frio! Mister Frio!"

Frio stepped to the ground and scooped the boy up in his arms, whirling him once around and putting him down again. "*Como le va,* Chico?"

Dark skin accented the sparkle of the boy's white teeth in a smile that was so wide it must have hurt.

"*Muy bueno.* Much good. This time you stay a while, no?"

Frio tousled the kid's black hair. "This time I stay a while *no*! Got to work. How is Señor McCasland? And Miss Amelia?"

The boy shrugged. "They not sick. Señor McCasland, he is work pretty hard. *La señorita*, she is worry what for you don't come a little quicker."

Frio dug a coin out of his pocket. "Go buy you some dulce."

The boy took the coin and shouted his thanks over his shoulder as he trotted barefoot off down the street, looking for a vendor. Frio walked inside the frame building and paused to let his sun-accustomed eyes adjust themselves to the interior. It was hot in here. Frio had heard it said that this country had summer nine months out of the year and late spring the other three.

Meade McCasland was showing some newly arrived English cloth to a couple of women customers. Once a strong man, he was breaking now with the weight of years and personal sorrow upon his broad shoulders. He saw Frio, and he said in a quiet Southern voice, "You ladies just take your time and look all you want to. I'll be right here." He strode forward and gripped Frio's hand so tightly it almost hurt.

"Glad to see you back, Frio. Have a good trip?"

Frio smiled, warming inside, for there was not a man alive he liked better than Meade McCasland. What little Frio could remember of his own father was reflected in this man. "It wasn't dull," he said and let it go at that. "Things seem to be bustlin' around here."

McCasland nodded. "More and more people coming in. Bookkeeper down at Kennedy & Co. said he saw more than a hundred ships anchored off Bagdad a few days ago. Every flag in Europe. A couple of Union blockaders were patrolling up and down like a pair of cats waiting at a mousehole, but there was nothing they could do about neutral vessels unloading on Mexican soil."

A thought came to Frio, unbidden: *They could take over Brownsville easy enough. That would stop it.* He didn't speak the thought. He knew it had come to

McCasland often enough anyway, and his friend had more troubles now than any two men ought to carry.

"You're lookin' well, Meade," he said, stretching the point a little. The old man didn't look good at all. "And Chico looks like you've been feedin' him all right."

Meade came close to smiling. "Chico never misses a meal." The boy's mother had worked for the McCaslands after her husband had been killed by *bandidos* on the Laredo road. When she had died of the fever and there had been no one else to care for the boy, Meade McCasland had taken the task upon his own shoulders.

Frio asked, "And Amelia? How's she?"

McCasland was plainly pleased that Frio asked. "She's back in the living quarters. She'd be up here now if she had any idea you had come in. I think she's been afraid you'd find some good-looking young lady in San Antonio."

Frio shook his head. "Never noticed they had any."

"They do. At least, they *did*. Never will forget the first time I was ever in San Antonio ..." Meade looked away, remembering. "But never mind that, just go on back. She'll be tickled to see you."

Frio walked through the door that separated the store from the dwelling in the rear of the building. Hat in hand, he closed the door quietly behind him. Amelia McCasland stood with her slender back turned. She and a young Mexican housegirl were holding up some unrolled new cloth, and Amelia was talking about what a lovely dress it was going to make. The widening of the housegirl's eyes caused Amelia to turn.

"Frio!" she cried, almost dropped the cloth. He saw joy leap in her pretty face, then confusion as she glanced back at the Mexican girl.

"Señorita," the girl said discreetly, "I will go on and start work in the kitchen."

"Yes, Consuela, please do that."

Frio stepped closer to Amelia as the girl left the room. Amelia smiled, "Well, come ahead, I'll let you kiss me."

He leaned down to give her a quick, unsure kiss. She caught his arm. "Not like that," she said. "Like this!" She tiptoed up and put her hands at his back and pulled him close. Her lips were warm and eager as they met his. In a moment she let her heels touch the floor again. She leaned back, her hands tight on his arms. Eyes sparkling, she said, "That's more like it. You going to ask me this time to marry you?"

Frio didn't know whether he ought to smile or frown. It seemed easier to smile. "Hadn't figured on it."

"And why not? Maybe if you'd ask me, I'd say yes."

"It seems to me you're the one who's proposing. I always thought that was for the man to do."

"It is, but you won't do it." Mischief was shining in her eyes. "Do you think I'm too forward, Frio?"

"Well, you're not the most bashful girl I ever met."

"I can't afford to be. Traveling as much as you do, you might meet somebody else. I've got to get you first." She watched him, waiting. "But, if you won't ask me this time, I'll just have to wait till the next trip, I guess. Sooner or later you're going to ask me."

Serious, he said, "Amelia, I've told you before: these trails can be dangerous. It's one thing to leave a sweetheart behind. It's another to leave a wife. Besides, I'm travelin' all the time. What kind of married life would that be for either one of us?"

The sparkle slowly went out of her eyes, and she went serious too. She leaned her body against him again, the side of her face pressed against his shoulder. "You'd be home once in a while—for a day, for a night. Better to have even so little than to have nothing at all."

It always seemed to Frio that Amelia had to work a little at her brashness. It served a purpose; to keep the sadness beaten back. But always the sadness lurked there somewhere, for this had been a tragic house.

"Better we wait a while yet, Amelia. Wait and see what the war is goin' to do." There was something more, something besides the war. She had lived all of her life in town. He wasn't sure how well she would fit on the ranch, especially during the early years when life there would necessarily lean toward the primitive. Not for all the money in the world would he have said so, but he was afraid she might not be able to take it. "Let's wait, Amelia," he said again.

"Until next time," she answered and put the subject aside. She motioned Frio toward a red-upholstered settee. "You were longer this time than usual."

"Took a while to get the government cotton together. Matter of fact, I had to leave ten of my wagons in San Antonio, waitin' for a load. Private speculators have been goin' around over the country, buyin' up cotton to try and make money on it. Government's had a hard time gettin' what it needs for the war trade."

Anger flared in Amelia's blue eyes. "Looks like the government could stop these speculators."

Frio shook his head. "Politics. Hard to catch them, and some have so much influence in Austin and Richmond that nobody can touch them anyway. Conscript law says anybody freightin' nongovernment cotton loses his exemption, but they don't enforce it much. War seems to breed its own brand of snakes."

They fell into silence. Frio liked just to sit and look at her. Gradually, though, his gaze drifted to a big charcoal drawing, framed and hanging on the wall. A Mexican artist across the river had done it just before the war. The likenesses were as real as a photograph: Meade McCasland, his wife and his daughter Amelia in the center, sons Tom on the left, Bert on the right.

On first thought it seemed to Frio that the artist had been kind to Meade, making him look much younger, leaving out the deep lines that had creased his face. But on reflection he knew the likeness had been real enough at the time. Most of the facial lines and much of the gray had come upon Meade since the war had started. He had suffered enough grief to kill some men.

Tennessee-born, McCasland had drifted to Texas in the 1830s and had fought beside Sam Houston at San Jacinto, avenging friends who died in the Alamo. He had come to the Rio Grande a few years after the Mexican War. He had loved his country, this sad-eyed man, and in the Texas secession referendum had voted like Sam Houston to keep Texas in the Union. But when the final count showed a majority for secession, McCasland had wept silently inside, then swallowed his bitter disappointment and accepted the Confederacy. His was a Southern heritage, and he would not stand against his friends.

Meade had not foreseen the split that was to come within his own family. In the echo of the guns at Fort Sumter, the youngest son Bert had marched off in gray to fight with the South. Tom, the older, remained fiercely loyal to the Union, quarreling even with his father. With others, Tom had tried to organize a resistance against the Confederacy in Texas. Failing, the militant Knights of the Golden Circle hard on his heels, he had retreated unwillingly across the river to sanctuary within the stone walls of Matamoros.

Mrs. McCasland fell easy prey to the fever, for she had lost the will to live. Bert was dead at Glorieta alongside so many others of Sibley's Brigade, and Tom was in exile beyond the Rio Grande. Meade McCasland was left with only his daughter.

Meade hadn't seen Tom in almost two years, though they were hardly more than a mile apart. Amelia crossed the river to visit him occasionally, for Tom held no bitterness against her.

It was in Frio's mind to tell Amelia what had happened to him on the trail, so that she might try to persuade Tom to stay on the south side of the Rio. He said, "You been across lately to see Tom?"

"I was there a couple of days ago, but I couldn't find him. He's been ... seeing a woman named Luisa Valdez. She was at his place. He was away on business, but he's well. She said we have nothing to worry about."

Nothing to worry about! A sour taste came to Frio's mouth. He realized that nothing Amelia could say would sway Tom much. No need to tell her and Meade McCasland that Tom's business had been north of the river, that it had been to ride with the *bandidos* of Florencio Chapa and attempt to destroy a wagon train.

Leaving, Frio found the happy Chico chewing candy on the front porch. The boy ran ahead and unhitched the sorrel for him.

Purely by chance, Frio overtook his wagon as he reined the horse away from the McCasland store and down the treelined dirt street. Blas Talamantes eyed him with a little surprise.

"You don't stay very long."

"Afraid I might say somethin' that had no need of bein' said."

They slanted down toward the big government cottonyard at the bend of the river. Beneath the dust of plodding hoofs and grinding wheels, he could see a thousand bales or more of CSA cotton. They were lined up awaiting sale and transshipment by rope ferry across to the Matamoros side, this to give them at least the cloak of legality and make them untouchable by the Yankee blockade ships. Across the river Frio could see one of the small shallow-draft steamers that belonged to M. Kennedy & Co. It was pulling in toward the Matamoros wharf, likely with a load of war goods freshly unloaded from some European ship anchored off Bagdad on the Mexican side of the river's mouth. The steamers had been signed over to Mexican owners and flew the eagle flag of Mexico, which was often referred to in joking disrespect as the Turkey Buzzard. But everyone knew this was only a wartime ruse, for the crews were the same as they had always been, and the original Texas owners still gave the orders.

Frio stopped the horse a moment to watch the boat and then let his gaze sweep downriver to where the Rio made another bend and was lost from sight. By land it was only thirty miles out to the gulf from Brownsville. By the river, with its leisurely snake-track course, it was nearer sixty. The flow was lower than usual because of the months of drought, and the little steamships had to pick their way cautiously past the sandbars and snags.

Frio wished he had time to ride out to the Boca Chica and watch the activity. He liked to go to the gulf and stand with wet boots on the salty beach at the river's mouth, watching rollers wash in tirelessly upon the land. He liked to look out across the blue waters at the white sails of the trading ships that rocked at anchor and imagine he could hear whispers from across the sea, beckoning whispers from strange lands he hadn't seen and never would. It always called up a wanderlust within him, a haunting wanderlust he would never be able to satisfy. He had never been out of Texas, except into Mexico, and he knew he would never go.

"Frio!"

Someone called his name, and he cut his eyes back to the cottonyard. He saw a heavyset, middle-aged man walking hurriedly toward him, a battered old felt hat pulled down over his eyes, an account book under his arm. Cotton agent Hugh Plunkett glanced at the trailing cotton wagon, then back to Frio.

"You all right, Frio?" he demanded. "Been worried half to death!"

Frio frowned, puzzled. "You knew we had trouble?"

Plunkett nodded vigorously, his gaze exploring up and down as if he were looking for bullet holes. "One of my Mexicans was over in Matamoros this mornin'. Saw some of Chapa's men come in with a big string of mules. They had your brand on them. I figured they'd killed you."

Frio's fist clenched. "Where'd they take the mules?"

"There's a sort of a wagonyard over there owned by Pablo Gutierrez, the fat one they call El Gordo."

Frio said, "I know him. Brother-in-law of Florencio Chapa, isn't he?"

Plunkett blinked. "Since you mention it, I believe he is."

Tightly Frio said, "It adds up. I bet you if I was to go over there, they'd sell me back my own mules."

"I wouldn't pay! I'd go and take my mules and kill the first man that opened his mouth!"

Frio glanced at the saddlegun on the sorrel and shook his head. "I admit it's a temptation. But we can't be raisin' any dust over in Mexico. I'll just have to swallow my medicine and act like it tastes good."

He told Hugh Plunkett about the raid and about losing some of the cotton.

Plunkett was sweating profusely, for a humid heat lay here along the river. "Frio, the cotton is the government's loss, but I'm afraid the wagon and the mules are yours. I wish there was somethin' I could do."

"There isn't, Hugh," Frio said regretfully. "Don't worry yourself."

Plunkett grunted angrily as a gust of hot wind slapped dust into his face from the passing of a high-wheeled Mexican ox-cart, loaded with cotton bales on their way down to the ferry. "Damn this river country anyway," he flared. The government had sent him here against his will, and he hadn't softened a bit. "We fought a war with the Mexicans once to take this country away from them. I say we ought to fight them again and make them take it back!"

Frio smiled and forgot his loss for a while. The cotton agent would probably still be griping when he got to Heaven, and nobody would think any more of it there than they did here. Frio handed Plunkett the manifests he had received with the cotton in San Antonio. Plunkett called up some of his help. They unloaded the bales from the lone wagon and checked them against the papers.

Frio said, "I'll go back and fetch in the rest of it soon as I get some mules to pull the wagons and a little lumber for patchin'."

Plunkett scowled. "You really goin' over there and buy back your mules?"

"I figure to try. They're good mules."

"I'd make somebody bleed for this."

"They will, Hugh." Frio's eyes narrowed. "Somebody is goin' to pay!"

As his empty wagon pulled out of the cottonyard, Frio swung into the saddle and looked around for Blas. Hugh Plunkett snapped his fingers, remembering something. "By the way, Frio, there's been a man lookin' for you. I oughtn't to even tell you."

"Who is it?"

"Cotton trader, that loudmouth Trammell."

The name brought a grunt from Frio, and a frown of distaste. "I got no business with that profiteer."

"I figure he wants to try to hire your wagons away from the government. Don't you let him do it, Frio."

Frio shook his head. "I'd as soon hire to Florencio Chapa. At least he admits to bein' a bandit."

3

FRIO AND BLAS LED their horses off the Santa Cruz ferry on the Mexican side and looked southward across the Estrero del Bravo to where the heart of Matamoros lay. About them bustled the river trade, cotton being unloaded from the ferry and carted up to yards to await shipment on the steamers. Mexican laborers and cotton buyers of many nationalities walked around among the dust-grayed bales stacked haphazardly here on the bank. Men shouted at each other and at their mules and oxen. Dust lifted and was slow to settle, for it had been a long time since rain.

The Gutierrez wagonyard lay southwestward, on the river. Frio swung into the saddle and started riding along the bank, Blas with him stirrup to stirrup. They passed a group of Mexican women washing clothes in the slow-moving water at river's edge. Frio wondered if the clothes would ever get clean.

A little farther, a group of girls bathed in the river, shouting and splashing. Some of them had few if any clothes on. Their wet brown skins gleamed in the sun.

"Now there," said Frio, "is a sight to gladden a man's heart."

Blas nodded and smiled and turned once to look back after they had passed the girls.

Matamoros! The formal Mexican name was much longer: *La Heroica y Invicta Ciudad de Matamoros*. The heroic and invincible. Named for a patriot priest who had died for Mexican freedom, this old border city had long known the smell of trouble, the sound and fury of war. Its time-stained walls were pocked with the marks of bullets and shells. Even now it was gripped by civil war, as was its sister city across the river, for the Indian patriot Juarez was locked in mortal combat with the imperialists and the French, who had proclaimed Maximilian emperor of all Mexico. Here in Matamoros seethed the same turmoil that had gripped the rest of the country, the Juarez Rojos opposing the Crinolinos, who supported Maximilian. At the moment the Crinolinos had control.

To most of the population there was always a war in progress, or just finishing, or just about to begin. They took it as a matter of course, like the droughts and the floods and the pestilence. Life would still go on after the armies had marched away. Commerce continued as if there were no struggle. Coins changed hands and the city grew, even as generals sparred and hapless soldiers gasped out their lives on bloody sand.

The trading circles spared little thought to politics.

Frio and Blas rode past the rude *jacales* that housed the poor. Half-naked children played in the dirt streets, and disheveled women cooked on outdoor ovens and open fires, sharing the food with the flies. These were tiny houses, the cots folding up against the walls in daytime to give what little room was to be had. Rapidly as the city had grown, these people were lucky to have even this, for many others lived with no roof at all.

Frio saw a big corral, started with rock but finished crudely with brush. "That would be it," he said.

They rode around the outside of the fence, looking in the corral at a motley collection of bone-poor horses and droopy-headed burros. There was no feed in the corral and only one tiny water trough, which now was half mud. Frio saw his mules, gaunted by the long, fast trip. They probably hadn't been fed at all, and they hadn't likely watered since they had been swum across the river. Anger stirred in him, but he curbed it. Here he would be doing the listening, not the talking.

He and Blas reined in at a low-built stone structure that was the Gutierrez headquarters. Several carts and sagging old wagons stood around in front of the building. An old *peón*, shoulders bent from a life of hard work, stepped out with his hat in his hand. He bowed from the waist. In Spanish he said, "How may I serve you, *patrón*?"

"I am looking for El G—" Frio caught himself. He had been about to say *El Gordo*, which in Spanish meant *the fat one* and was not usually a term of endearment. "I would like to speak to Señor Gutierrez."

The *peón* hesitated. Frio added, "It is on business. I would like to buy some mules from him."

"Then," said the old man, "if you will step inside, *mi jefe* will be most glad to see you." There was a nervousness about the old man, an undertone of fear. Likely as not that tattered old shirt covered whip scars on his bent back. Here a rich man like El Gordo could virtually own a poor man, much as across the river a white man could own a black one.

The *peón* walked cautiously through a door and closed it quietly behind him. Frio could hear a voice in angry impatience, demanding what the old man wanted. In a moment El Gordo Gutierrez stepped through the door, his belly sagging, his mouth wide in a false smile. His eyes smiled too, in anticipation of profit. Gutierrez didn't seem even to see Blas Talamantes. He ignored him as an *hidalgo* might ignore another man's *peón* grubbing in the dirt. He bowed from the waist, which was something of an effort for him, and said to Frio, "My house is yours, señor. Tell me how I may serve you, and I shall be the happiest of men."

Frio sensed that Gutierrez knew him. He was glad the man didn't extend his hand, for he wasn't sure he could have brought himself to shake it. "I need to buy some mules. Thought maybe you had some for sale."

"Ahhh." Gutierrez rubbed his hands. "You are indeed a fortunate man, señor, for it happens I have just brought in a large group of mules from one of the best ranches in Mexico. I would be glad to show you." He motioned toward a back door, which would lead to the big corral. Frio stepped toward it, then stopped as he glanced into the room from which Gutierrez had come. Two men slouched at a table, a bottle sitting in front of them. Frio stiffened. One of them was the *bandido*, Florencio Chapa. Chapa sat watching him, amusement playing in his black eyes. His was a cruel face that could grin while his hands cut a man's throat.

The other man was, in his own way, even more dangerous than Chapa. This was General Juan Nepomuceno Cortina, the wily political opportunist whose brigandage had been carried out on such a high plane as to keep him in a position of power no matter which political party might be gaining the edge in Mexico. Born of aristocratic blood but hardly able to write his own name, he was the beloved "Cheno" Cortina to most of the Mexican people—Cheno the gringo-killer, the champion of Mexican rights against the encroachment of the Anglos. And if somehow Cortina seemed always to have gained more for himself than for his followers, that was of no matter. He was Cheno, and he deserved whatever good there was to be gained from life.

"This way, señor," Gutierrez said, holding the door open.

Frio stepped out into the sun, Blas following him. Frio glanced back over his shoulder, thinking he might again glimpse Cortina. This was the man who had taken a hundred followers across the river one early morning in 1859 and had captured Brownsville by storm, summarily executing five men—some of them Mexicans—who had earned his wrath. It took a Mexican general, Carvajal, to get Cortina out of Brownsville. It took the Texas Rangers under old Rip Ford to drive him back across the river. Even afterward, he kept crossing the Rio Grande to raid small *ranchos*, taking vengeance not only on Anglos but on the Mexicans who worked for them. He had been chased by the best of men, including even Robert E. Lee, who at the time had still been a lieutenant colonel in the U.S. Army.

Frio thought this red-bearded, gray-eyed highbinder probably was enjoying the war between the states, the thought of gringo killing gringo, with Cortina able to sit back and make money out of it through the cotton trade. Though he plied his banditry in higher and more sophisticated circles now, the love of it still burned in him, and he encouraged such savage *bandidos* as Chapa and the notorious Octaviano Zapata.

Gutierrez said, "You would like to meet Cheno? He's one good friend of mine."

Frio shook his head. "No, thank you. I'd rather just get on with our business." He knew he was rushing too much. Mexicans liked to take their time on a business transaction, to talk all around it as if it were not even there. But Frio didn't think he could stand to be in El Gordo's presence for very long. He wanted to rush it, to get it over with.

There was no mistake about their being his mules. He would have recognized them anywhere, even without the brands. If there had been any point in his demonstrating this, he could have popped a whip and shouted an order, and they would have moved into their places, ready to harness. The Mexican *caporal* had taught him that, to save time in breaking camp and getting the wagons out on the trail.

Smiling, Gutierrez said, "They are fine-looking mules. They would do a good job for your freight wagons."

That was the clincher. Frio knew for certain now that El Gordo was well aware of who he was. "I know they would," Frio remarked. "They're my mules."

"Your mules?" El Gordo put on an act of not understanding. "They are *my* mules. I bought them." His eyes smiled again. "But they can be your mules if you like. I would be glad to sell them."

I'll just bet you would, Frio thought, having to curb his anger again. "How much?"

The Mexican looked at the ground and rubbed his hands. "They are unusually good mules. Seldom does one see better. I would say they are worth a hundred dollars per head."

"Confederate?"

El Gordo violently shook his head. "Not Confederate money. Gold."

"I'll give you seventy-five, Confederate."

From there on it was simply a process of dickering and bargaining. El Gordo had set the original price at double what he expected to get. After a while they arrived at an agreement. Fifty dollars per head, payable in English paper. That much gold would take a wagon. The harness, some of it cut, would be thrown in free.

"Bueno," said El Gordo, "we shall drink on it."

They went back inside. Chapa and Cortina had gone. Gutierrez got two dry glasses and a bottle of tequila, deliberately ignoring Blas Talamantes. Frio handed his own glass to Blas and thus forced El Gordo to get a third one.

"To your health, señor," El Gordo said. "May we have more pleasant business together."

We're going to have a little more business, Frio thought darkly, *but you may not think it's so pleasant.*

He emptied the glass in one long swallow. It was harsh, leaving a deep track all the way down.

"Come on, Blas," he said. "We'll need to find some men and come after the mules. And I have to get the money for Señor Gutierrez."

They left the yard and rode toward the heart of the city. Frio looked once over his shoulder. "Blas," he said after some deliberation, "I guess you know a lot of people in this town."

They had just passed a nice-looking girl seated in the big window of one of the better homes, leaning against the wrought-iron grating. Blas glanced back at her and said, *"Sí,* Frio, but all that has changed. I am married now. María is all the woman I need."

"You misunderstand me, Blas. I was just wonderin' if you might know five or six jolly Mexican boys who might like to pull a good honest robbery."

Blas smiled broadly as comprehension came. "*Sí*, Frio. I think maybeso."

"Do it, then. I'll go to the British consul and get the money. Then I'll wait in that little bar down from the consulate till you show up. Tell them I'll let them keep a hundred apiece if they do the job right."

Blas started to turn away, then stopped. Worry creased his face. "One thing, Frio. You never can tell. Maybe they run away and keep it all."

"A chance I'll take. I wouldn't be any worse off than I am now."

Here on the border, where the trade was heavy, gold was not hard to come by. For more than a year now Frio had insisted upon foreign currency or gold in payment for his government hauling. Stern realism dictated the measure. Even here on the border, people were trading two dollars of Confederate paper money for one in gold. From things he had heard in San Antonio he knew they were swapping as many as four to one in the deep South. As long as the gold was available, he would take it. Everyone on the border did.

Because it would be easy for the Yankees to sail up to the Brazos Santiago or the Boca Chica one day and march in to capture Brownsville, he could not afford to keep his money in Texas. There was as yet no trustworthy bank in Matamoros, but an English cotton buyer had helped Frio work out an arrangement with the British consul. Frio could keep a supply of floating cash at the consulate and could send the rest by draft to a bank in England.

English money was acceptable at face value in Matamoros because so much of it was used in buying cotton. Frio drew out two thousand dollars—the equivalent of it—for the forty mules. Carrying it in a small bag, he strolled down the street to the bar where he had said he would meet Blas. There he ordered a good Scotch whisky, which arrived there now aboard the trading ships, and hunted a place to sit down. He put his back to a solid wall. With all this money on his person, he didn't care to be slipped up on.

From here he could see the cosmopolitan parade of humanity that passed the door—cotton buyers and merchants from England and France, Belgium and Germany; sailors from vessels of many nations, delayed at the Boca Chica by repairs; Texans who had come to Mexico because of pro-Union feelings, or simply to escape the draft; Negro slaves who had fled from bondage. There were even federal observers sent here from Washington to keep a futile watch over the border trade. They knew what was going on but were powerless to put even a small dent in it.

A man could sit in one spot here on the main streets of Matamoros for just a day, and half the world would pass before him.

In the main, it seemed to Frio, Matamoros was still a more solid-looking town than Brownsville. It was larger, had more fine homes, had most of the better eating and drinking places and the only real theater. One had to overlook the fringe of primitive *jacales* and tents and open-air campers who had swelled the city of late. One also had to overlook the many cheap cantinas and gambling places and rowdy sporting houses that had sprung up to accommodate the flush pockets of freighters and sailors and traders, Confederate soldiers and plain salt-sweat laborers.

Two men entered the bar and ordered drinks. One of them spotted Frio, spoke quickly to the other, then began walking in Frio's direction. He was a portly man with florid face and eyes that somehow reminded Frio of a coyote's. The clothes he wore had been well tailored and bespoke easy money, but now they looked as if he might have slept in them.

"Hello, Frio Wheeler," he said loudly, as if he had found a long-lost friend. He walked up and slapped Frio's shoulder with a big soft hand. "Been hopin' I'd run into you someplace."

Frio's voice lacked enthusiasm. "Hello, Trammell." He didn't offer to shake.

Trammell hailed the other man with a broad sweep of his hand. "Guffey, come over here. I want you to meet the best cotton freighter on the whole Mexico trail."

Frio didn't stand up nor did he offer his hand to the tall, consumptive-looking Guffey. Trammell was telling him Guffey was a cotton buyer out of New York—strictly nonpolitical—but Frio only half listened. He already knew Guffey by sight and reputation. Trammell said in his big, loud voice, "How about havin' a drink with us, Frio?"

It graveled Frio a little, this careless use of his first name. In his view that was a privilege granted only to friends. He did not count Trammell as a friend. "I've already got a drink. Thanks anyway." He hoped this might discourage Trammell and that the man would go away. Instead, Trammell scraped a chair across the floor and seated himself uninvited. "Let's sit down here, Guffey. I got some business I want to talk over with Frio."

Frostily Frio said, "We got no business together."

"You don't know it, but we do."

A waiter brought a bottle and two glasses. Trammell poured a glass full and swallowed it down in two long gulps. His face twisted sourly, and he rasped a long "Ahhhh!" Across the table, the lank Guffey only sipped at the whiskey, his nose wrinkling as if he smelled something dead. Frio scowled, looking the two men over, sorely tempted to get up and walk out but realizing Blas wouldn't know where to hunt for him.

Here's a real pair for you, he thought. Trammell was a trader who had gotten fat buying cotton from poor farmers in East Texas and selling it to the Confederacy at high prices. It had been charged but never proven that he bribed government buyers to give him a premium. Now he had found there was even more cream to be skimmed by not dealing with the Confederacy at all, but by hauling his cotton to the border and selling it directly to the buyers from overseas. That way it wound up to his credit in European banks. None of it had to be traded for war goods.

As for Guffey, he was a Yankee cotton buyer. How he did it Frio could only guess, but Guffey actually was getting his hands on arms and ammunition that were being manufactured for the Union army. He was shipping them to Matamoros and trading them to the Confederate government in return for cotton, which he could sell at ruinous prices to fiber-hungry mills in the east.

The .36-caliber Navy Colt that Frio carried on his belt had been Union war goods that had come through Guffey's hands.

Trammell set his glass down with a hard thump. "Frio, how would you like to make yourself a big pile of money? Good gold money that spends anywhere you want to take it."

"I'm doin' all right."

"Join up with me, man, and you'll make more than you'll know how to spend. You could buy yourself the best ranch in Mexico and have all the pretty señoritas a man could ever want, a different one for every day."

Frio could feel color rising warm in his cheeks. His narrowed eyes fastened on his glass to avoid looking at Trammell. "That might be to your taste. It isn't to mine."

"Just a figure of speech is all. Hell, money's to everybody's taste. You can do anything you want to with it."

Frio said, "Bad money breeds only trouble, and yours is bad money. I don't want any part of it."

Trammell stared incredulously. "There's no such thing as bad money. All I want you to do is haul my cotton. You're a good freighter, and you've got fifteen good wagons."

"Fourteen," Frio corrected him. "Lost one."

"Haul for me and you can have thirty wagons before you know it. I'll pay you twice what the government does."

Frio shook his head. "Not interested."

Trammell argued, "Look, man, I got more than four thousand bales of cotton bought in East Texas. Bought cheap. They stand to make me a fortune if I can get them down to the border. I'll split the profit with you if you'll haul them. Now, what could be more fair than that?"

"Sell them to the government."

"Sell ... Man, you're crazy! I'm offerin' you a chance to make a small fortune, and you sit here starin' at me like some dumb Mexican." The big man grabbed Frio's shoulder and shook it. "Think of all that cotton, Frio. Think what I've got tied up in it. Think of me!"

Frio's hating gaze cut him like a knife. "I am thinkin' of you, Trammell, and the thought makes me a little bit sick. You take cotton the Confederacy needs and sell it for gold to line your own pockets. Now take your hand off of me before I shoot it off!"

Trammell jerked his hand away.

Frio turned to the Yankee. "And you, Guffey, you're just as bad. Sure, the Confederacy needs all the guns it can get. But I mortally hate a man who would steal from his own side and sell guns to the enemy, even when we're the enemy."

Trammell sputtered, "You got no call to talk to us like that, Frio. We come for a nice, friendly little business talk and you—"

"I didn't invite you," Frio said flatly. "But now I'm invitin' you to leave. In fact, I'm tellin' you to."

Trammell backed toward the door, shaking his fist. "You'll regret this, Wheeler. We'll meet again."

"As long as I can see you," Frio said, "I won't be worried."

Blas came, bye and bye. He simply stood in the doorway and nodded, and Frio knew everything had been arranged. Walking outside, he saw half a dozen Mexicans a-horseback, waiting. Blas said, "I hire these to help us put the mules across the river."

"And that other little job?"

Blas winked. "I have fix that also."

They rode out to Gutierrez's. Frio placed the money in the big man's greedy hands and watched gold-lust dance in the dark eyes. The Mexicans harnessed the mules, then strung them out along the river, headed for the ferry.

Riding off behind the mules, Frio and Blas passed a tall stone fence and found four young Mexicans sitting there on their horses, waiting. They made no sign of recognition, but Frio saw Blas give them a quick nod as he rode by. Frio looked back over his shoulder a minute later and saw them riding leisurely toward the wagonyard.

After taking his mules to the Texas side, Frio rode the ferry back to Matamoros and returned once more to the bar near the consulate. He hadn't been there long when Blas came, bringing the same bag in which Frio had taken the money to Gutierrez.

"Did they take out their share?" he asked, not wanting to open the bag here.

Blas nodded. "Funny thing. When they rob him they find he has more money there than you give him. They take their share from El Gordo's money. You will find yours here, all of it."

Frio smiled, then suddenly the smile fell away. "El Gordo . . . I hope they didn't kill him."

Blas shook his head. "No, they don't kill him. One of the boys, he's make El Gordo saddle a horse, and he's take him for a long ride down the river. He's going to let El Gordo walk back."

Frio could picture Gutierrez wobbling along afoot, carrying his great bulk on legs unaccustomed to walking.

"He'll know who arranged it, of course."

Blas shrugged. "Of course, but what can he do? You know who is steal your mules, but what could *you* do?"

Frio laughed all the way back to the consulate.

4

FRIO KNEW WHERE TOM McCasland lived in Matamoros, but he had never gone there to look for him before. Now and again he and Tom would meet by accident somewhere in the city. They were always civil meetings, but inevitably the barrier of war and the conflict of loyalties stood like a stone wall between the two men. Such meetings only aroused in Frio a painful memory of things that used to be—the hunting and fishing they had done together, horses they had broken, cattle work with the two of them and Blas Talamantes as a happy team. With these memories always came a fear that when the war ended, that friendship would never again be the same. Always when he saw Tom, Frio felt an aching sense of loss. He avoided a meeting if he had the chance.

This time he felt he had to see Tom, had to try to talk sense.

Frio knocked at the door of the small frame house. For a moment he thought there would be no answer, then he heard someone walking softly. The door opened just a little, and dark eyes peered out cautiously. A woman's eyes.

"*Quién es?*" she asked suspiciously.

Frio removed his hat. "I'm lookin' for Tom McCasland."

"He is not here. Go away." She closed the door.

Frio rapped again. The door opened once more, a little wider this time. She was a Mexican woman in her mid-twenties—not a beauty, perhaps, but more than passable—and she was angry. "Look," she said in English that was surprisingly good, "I tell you already, he is not home. He has ride for you already one time this week. Why you don't leave him alone?"

"You got me mixed up with somebody else, ma'am. I'm a friend of his. I just want to talk with him."

The door opened a little wider. "You come to talk war? I don't want for him to ride out anymore. Next time they kill him maybe."

"I don't want him to ride out anymore either. That's what I came to talk to him about."

The anger began to fade from her eyes. "You are not another of those from the *Yanqui* government, wanting him to do the dangerous things?"

Frio shook his head. "I'm from *el otro lado*, the other side of the river. Name's Frio Wheeler."

"Wheeler." She frowned, slowly testing the word on her tongue. "Yes, I have hear him speak that name. You are a friend."

"I used to be. I hope I still am."

The door swung open. "Tom is not here, Señor Wheeler. But come in. Maybe we should talk together."

The room was not cool, for she had kept the front

door closed against intrusion from the foot traffic on the street. He felt some flow of air through open side windows and a back door. The room was simply furnished, nothing fancy. He saw curtains, though, and a bowl of cut flowers adding a splash of color. Tom wasn't living here by himself.

"I haven't met you before," Frio said.

She had a handsome figure, and from the lightness of her complexion he thought she might be pure Spanish. There was still pride in the people of the *sangre puro*, the unmixed blood. He sensed that she was a lady, or had been.

"I am Luisa Valdez."

She would have stopped there, but Frio glanced at her hand and saw the rings. Then she went on, for his eyes were asking the question he was too polite to speak. "Yes, I am a married woman, or was. My husband is one time an officer for the Juaristas. The Crinolinos, they kill him. Tom McCasland, he is good friend of my husband and me. When my husband is die, I have no people anymore, no money. For a woman without these things, there is but one way to live in Matamoros. I would die first. So I am come to Tom, and he is give me a place to live." She paused. "I know what you think, but he is a good man."

Frio said, "I know that, ma'am, a good man." He twisted his hat. "You in love with him?"

She was slow to answer. Then, nodding, she replied, "Yes, I love him."

"You figurin' on marryin' him?"

She dropped her chin. "He has ask me, and I am tell him no. I love him, Señor Wheeler, but war has make me a widow one time. I do not want that it makes me a widow again. I tell Tom that when his war is over, when there is no more fight, then I marry him. Not before that. I do not want to be widow ever again."

"I wouldn't want you to be. I want to have Tom stay in Matamoros where he won't be gettin' hurt. You know where he's at right now?"

She shook her head. "He is tell me he has government business. He says he will be back tonight and take me to the *fandango*."

Frio had heard something about the big dance while he was sitting in the bar waiting for Blas. "You think if I went to the *fandango* I'd get a chance to see him?"

"He will be there."

Frio said, "Then so will I."

He started to back toward the door. Luisa Valdez stared at him with eyes that seemed to weep for sadness. She shifted to Spanish because the words came easier to her that way. "Señor Wheeler, there is much I do not understand. Where is there reason in all this war? You and Tom, you are friends, but one of you is on one side and one is on the other. You are friends and yet you are enemies. Where is there reason in this?"

He answered her in English, for though he understood Spanish well enough, he could not always express himself as he wanted. It was common on the border to hear bilingual conversations, each party using the language that came easiest. "Well, Mrs. Valdez, it's this way. . . ." His voice trailed off, for he knew he couldn't explain it to her. He couldn't explain it to himself.

"War," she said gravely, "is a useless thing, a foolishness that men create for themselves. They fight wars like they would race horses or gamble with cards or put roosters in a pit. It is the woman who suffers, because she must live on alone when her man has died. The men fight, but it is the women who must cry the tears and live an empty life after the foolish game of the men is over. If it were left to the women, there would be no wars."

Frio tried to meet her accusing gaze but looked away. There was no arguing with her, because he could find no answer for what she had said.

"You are a soldier?" she asked him.

He shook his head. "No, I am a rancher and a freighter. I freight cotton to the river and haul merchandise north."

"You are not a soldier, but your wagons carry the goods that go to fight the war. Is there really a difference?"

"Not much," he admitted, "when you think about it. But it's somethin' somebody has to do, and it seems I'm the one. Our side didn't ask for this war, ma'am. It was somethin' they forced us to."

Her eyes seemed to pity him. "I suppose the other side feels the same way about it."

Frio dropped his gaze. "I hadn't done much thinkin' on it thataway."

"It is how Tom feels. Strange, isn't it? Both of you feel the same way, yet you find yourselves on opposite sides, against each other. Perhaps both of you need to do some thinking. Perhaps each of you could see the other's viewpoint if you tried."

Uncomfortable, completely out of answers, Frio found himself edging again toward the door. This was no ordinary woman, he could see that. Luisa Valdez had a mind of her own, a strong one.

He said, "Tell Tom, will you, that I'll see him at the *fandango*. No, on second thought, don't tell him. He might not go."

"He will go," she promised. "I will see to it."

He stepped outside. He started to put his hat on and walk toward the sorrel, but he turned back to Luisa Valdez. "Hang on to him, Mrs. Valdez, and keep him out of trouble. I'd like to see you married to him. I'd like to have you for a friend."

Her lips turned upward with a thin semblance of a smile. "*Ojalá*. You are a good man too, I think. I would hope we can be friends."

The Matamoros *fandango* was more than a dance. It was a meeting place for friends who hadn't seen each other in a long time. It was a whole-family affair and a drinking bout and a gamblers' haven, all rolled into one. It wouldn't get started until nine o'clock, because darkness wouldn't come until after eight. The last of the diehards wouldn't leave before daylight had come again.

Frio went back on the ferry to the Brownsville side to bathe and shave and put on fresh clothes. He also took the opportunity to be sure his recovered mules had been given plenty of feed and fresh water. They had already taken on a good fill by the time he saw them. Tomorrow or the next day they would be ready for the trail.

He dropped by the McCasland place to visit a little more with Meade, and to see Amelia again. Amelia's eyes widened when he told her where he was going tonight. "The *fandango*? What do you want to go there for?"

"For one thing, they're fun. For another, I've got some business."

Her eyes narrowed. "What kind of business? What does she look like?"

Frio tried to keep his face serious. "Well, she stands about six-and-a-half feet tall, has one blue eye and one brown one. Get tired of one color, you just look at the other eye awhile."

"I'm green with jealousy." Excitement kindled in her face. "Frio, I've never been to a *fandango*. Take me with you."

"Amelia, a *fandango* across the river isn't like the dances you see over here. They're not what you're used to."

"That suits me fine," she said eagerly. "I've heard about them, but I've never had anyone to take me. I certainly couldn't go by myself. Now I've got somebody to go with, and I want to see one." Her eyes were aglow. She squeezed his hands. "Please, Frio."

"I'll level with you, Amelia. Main reason I'm goin' is to have a talk with Tom."

"I'd like to see him too."

"What we've got to talk about, you might not like."

Her eyes changed. She seemed to sense that something was not right. "You're friends, Frio. I hope you're not going to argue with him again about the war."

"Not the whole war, Amelia, just a little part of it."

"I still want to go."

He gave in grudgingly. "All right," he acceded, against his better judgment. "I'll be back about eight and get you. I'll borrow a rig."

Later he asked Blas Talamantes if he was going. Blas shook his head. María was at the ranch, Blas explained, and a dance wouldn't mean much without her. It had been only three days since Blas had left the ranch, but already he was homesick for his wife.

Amelia's face was aglow with adventure as Frio slowed the buggy horse to a walk in the heavy traffic around the Matamoros main plaza. The smell of flowers and the sound of music were in the air. Young

couples strolled arm in arm along the fenced walk-
ways that led inward toward the center circle of the
plaza like spokes slanting to the hub of a wheel. Old
men—and those not yet old but married long enough
to enjoy getting away from their women—sat on
benches beneath the trees to tell lies about their
exploits in war and on the perilous trails.

Amelia looked up in the gathering darkness at the
two tall spires of the huge cathedral that sat beside the
American-looking customs house. "A beautiful thing,
isn't it?" she said. "Even when they were hungry, they
took from what little money they had and built a
church."

"The soul," said Frio, quoting a Mexican priest he
had heard, "may hunger more than the body."

Listening in the night, he could hear voices speaking many tongues—Spanish and English, naturally,
but French and German as well, and others he could
not identify. All these people, drawn from across the
world to this unlikely place by the smell of money—
and the money because of war.

His mind went back to the sorrow he had seen in the
dark eyes of Luisa Valdez. "It's a soul-hungry time,"
he said.

Paper lanterns of many colors spread their light on
the hundreds who were drawn to the gaiety of the *fandango*. By nine-thirty most of the crowd was there.
Somewhere off to one side, boys were firing squibs
and firecrackers, and frightened horses jerked at the
reins that held them to a fence.

The little orchestra began to play. It was made up of
an old fiddle, an ancient clarinet, and a drum, the latter
nothing but a barrel with rawhide stretched across the
top. There was a guitar and a trumpet. Leader was Don

Sisto the fiddler, a stoop-shouldered old man with gray mustache and fiercely proud eyes, and a leather outfit that must once have been something to see. Like its wearer, it had been too many miles down too many roads.

Her hand clasped on Frio's arm, Amelia McCasland walked about, fascinated by what she saw. Always there had been a quiet admiration and a soft spot in her heart for the Mexicans. Benches had been placed in such a manner as to form a large square. Dancers used the center area while spectators sat on the benches. Many of the Mexican women smoked, just as did their men. Amelia watched in wonder. Across the river it was not unusual for Texas women to dip snuff, but she had never seen them smoke. Well, almost never. Now and again she had seen an immigrant Southern woman—not of the gentry—smoke a corncob pipe.

Outside the benches, gambling tables and drinking booths had been set up. Frio didn't count them, but he guessed there must have been forty tables, most already occupied by games of monte. The players bent in intense concentration. Men, women, and even a goodly number of children stood around the outer fringes, watching the monte with as much eagerness as did the players themselves.

A sudden stir began at the entrance. Frio saw a bright-colored uniform and the proud bearing of the man who wore it. A worshipful retinue followed along with the officer. Even the monte players looked up, and many of the people began to cheer.

Amelia squeezed Frio's arm. "Is that who I think it is?"

He nodded. "It's Cortina—the Red Robber of the Rio Grande."

She said quickly, "Shh-h-h, don't talk that way.

You're in his country now." She stared at the fabled Mexican officer. "So that's what he really looks like. He isn't nearly so big as I thought he was the other time I saw him."

Surprised, Frio asked, "When was that?"

"The time he took Brownsville four years ago. It was one morning before daylight. I heard horses running and people yelling. There were some shots. I ran to the window just as a Mexican loped by shouting, 'Viva Cheno Cortina! Death to the gringos!' Then came Cortina himself, riding at the head of a group. It was dark, so I couldn't see him clearly, but he looked seven feet tall there in the saddle. Dad pulled me away from the window then. He and Tom and Bert kept me hidden in the cellar until Cortina and his men all left town."

Frio noticed that the music had slowed. Don Sisto had turned to see what the excitement was about, and his face had tightened with sudden anger. Though most Mexicans revered Cortina, Don Sisto was one of that minority who hated him with passion. Once Cortina's raiders had picked up Don Sisto and his band on the Brownsville-Laredo road, thinking them to be Texas-Mexican government officials. They had carried the men to Cortina to see if he wanted them shot. "Damned musicians!" Cortina had shouted impatiently. "*Fandango* sharps! Turn them loose and get them out of here!"

The insult had given Don Sisto's pride a wound that would never heal. "He did not need to treat us as if we were dogs," he had said a hundred times. "The least he could have done was to shoot us like men!"

Cortina's eyes touched Frio for a moment, recognizing him. Then the border chieftain found himself a seat at a table, the worshiping retinue crowding around him. Don Sisto went back to his music.

Frio said to the girl, "If you've had enough, I'll take you home."

"Not on your life," she thrilled. "I wouldn't have missed this for all of Abe Lincoln's gold."

He had looked all around the place and hadn't seen any sign of Tom. "Amelia, I'm no great shakes as a dancer, but I'd be much obliged if you'd try one with me."

He found the girl light and graceful in his arms. Though he was wooden and unpracticed at this, she seemed to follow along without a bobble, making him feel like a good dancer. They danced one tune, two tunes, three. Each one was faster than the one before it. When the last tune ended, Frio was puffing.

"I'm about caved in," he grinned, not really wanting to quit. He enjoyed having her in his arms. "Maybe we better set a spell."

Amelia didn't seem to have tired a bit. Her eyes aglow, she laughed, "Who was it said this would be too tough for me?"

He took her hand and led her back toward the benches. He stopped abruptly as he saw Tom McCasland standing there with Luisa Valdez. Tom's face was sober, but Frio could tell it wouldn't take much prompting to cause him to smile.

Tom stepped forward and kissed his sister. "Hello, Sis. Never dreamed I'd see you here."

Amelia looked him up and down critically, as if worried about his health. "Found out Frio was coming. You couldn't have driven me away with a club."

Hesitantly Tom extended his hand. "Hello, Frio."

"Howdy, Tom." Frio gripped his old friend's hand, and for a moment they stood looking at one another, searching each other's eyes to see if the old friendship had survived the years. It had.

Tom said, "I believe you've both met Luisa."

Frio bowed from the waist. Amelia nodded her head but stared uncertainly at Mrs. Valdez. She was plainly at a loss as to how she should accept the woman. There could be no doubt in her mind about the relationship between Luisa Valdez and her brother. It was a relationship that would have brought censure across the river. Here it seemed to be taken as a matter of course. Recognizing that she was south of the river and that it was not her place to pass judgment, Amelia said courteously, "It's nice to see you again, Luisa."

And Luisa Valdez, undoubtedly reading everything that passed through Amelia's mind, replied with all the grace of one to the manor born. "And you, Amelia. You are most pretty tonight."

Tom said, "I see an empty table over yonder. I've brought some brandy."

They sat, and Tom poured brandy into four small glasses. The two men and Mrs. Valdez sipped theirs with pleasure. Amelia went slowly, tasting with caution. For a proper young woman on the Texas side of the river, not even brandy was lightly taken. She had sampled little of it in her life.

Amelia and Tom talked of personal things, about life in Brownsville, about their father and his store. Finally Tom looked back to Frio. "Luisa said you wanted to talk to me. I can make a fair guess what it's about."

Frio glanced at Amelia. "Might be better if we went off someplace, Tom, just us two."

"If it's about the war, there's no use startin'."

"Not the whole war, Tom, just your part in it."

Tom shrugged. "There's not much to tell. I'm

workin' for the United States government through Leonard Pierce, the consul. I keep watch, make reports about the border situation, the river trade and such."

Frio's eyes narrowed. "Does that job include goin' across the river?"

Amelia stiffened in surprise. Luisa Valdez was staring down into her brandy, her face grave.

Tom said, "What do you mean by that?"

Frio glanced at Amelia and wondered if he ought to say it. But she would find out sooner or later. "Tom, I lost four teams of mules, a wagon, and some cotton. One of my men was wounded. Blas Talamantes and me, we were in the brush and saw the raiders as they came by."

Tom lowered his head, "And?"

"And I want to know why, Tom. What's the sense of it? With all the hundreds of wagons that come down the trail, what good would it do you to knock out five, or even ten or fifteen? It's like tryin' to empty the Gulf of Mexico with a bucket."

Tom put his hands together and thoughtfully pressed his thumbs against his chin. "I didn't know they were your wagons, Frio, till we got there and I saw your brand painted on them. It wouldn't have made any difference, though, it had to be done." His eyes asked for understanding. "Frio, I love Texas as much as you do. I don't want to kill anybody. The way I see it, you don't have to kill a man to stop him; you can scare him away. If we hit a few wagons here, a few there, we can scare a lot of teamsters. We can make them afraid to start down the trail. Get enough men scared and we can slow down the border trade. Might even stop it."

"When a man's fightin' for what he believes in, he

can take a lot of scarin' and still go on. What if they don't stop, Tom?"

Tom's face pinched with regret. "Then I guess we'll have to kill."

Frio stared awhile at his old friend, knowing that at heart Tom was as sick of the war as he was himself. "Look at the caliber of men you're ridin' with, Tom. Florencio Chapa, a cutthroat. His own people are afraid of him. Even Cortina hates him, though he uses him. And Bige Campsey! Now, there's a renegade for you."

"War forces a man into some strange partnerships, Frio. We need Chapa, and he's available, so we use him."

"Maybe it's the other way around; maybe he's usin' you. He's a born murderer. I could name you a dozen helpless Mexican teamsters he's tortured to death on the old Laredo road. All you've done is give him a chance to kill and claim it's legal. He rides out now and carries an American flag with him. No flag means anything to Chapa; not the Mexican flag and surely not yours."

Tom said, "He didn't kill anybody on this raid. That's one reason I went along, to be sure he didn't kill anybody he didn't have to. As for Campsey, he's loyal to the Union and wants to fight. He came here because he couldn't accept the Confederacy."

Frio said sharply, "He couldn't accept the draft. He came here because he shot a conscript officer in cold blood."

He could tell by the surprise in Tom's face that this was news to him. "This kind of business takes rough men, Frio."

Frio begged, "Quit this, Tom, while you still can.

One day they'll catch you across the river and you won't get back."

Tom slowly shook his head. "I know what I have to do, Frio. I've argued with you before about the Union and the Confederacy, so I won't do that now. Each of us has his own loyalties, and nothin' we say to each other will change that. But I want you to think, Frio. One day soon the Union is goin' to send troops in here and close this border. Nothin' you can do will alter that. The trail's goin' to be dangerous from now on. I wish you'd go back to that ranch of yours and stay there. This war won't last much longer. I want you to be alive when it's over."

"What makes you think you're goin' to win?"

"You may not have gotten the news yet, Frio. Have you heard about Gettysburg?"

Frio shook his head. "Who is he?"

"It's not a man, it's place, a town in Pennsylvania. They've just fought a big battle there, the worst of the war. No one knows how many men died. When it was over, Lee and his army fell back toward Virginia. The Union will win now. It's just a question of time." His eyes pleaded. "See, Frio? There's no use for you to risk your life anymore. Your cause is lost."

Shaken by Tom's news, Frio still could not accept it, *would* not accept it. "It can't be. We've hoped so long, struggled so hard. . . ." He looked up. "A man doesn't accept defeat while he still stands. He fights as long as the breath is still in him. Stop my wagons? No, sir! I'll patch them and try to buy more. I'll haul cotton south as long as there's anybody to buy it, and I'll haul war supplies north as long as there's anybody left to haul them to. Quit? Hell, man, I haven't even started yet!"

Tom's eyes went cold in disappointment. "You may die, Frio."

"It'll be in the service of Texas."

Tom said softly, "I'm in the service of Texas too. I'm servin' her the way it seems best to me."

He looked up at the sound of angry voices. Frio turned in his chair. He saw El Gordo Gutierrez limping painfully toward him, his face livid with rage, his hands a-tremble. Beside him stalked the black-clad *bandido*, Florencio Chapa.

"You are a thief!" El Gordo bawled at Frio, his finger pointing. "You have taken my mules and stolen my money!"

The sight of the fat man somehow broke Frio's somber mood. Incredibly, he wanted to laugh. El Gordo's clothes were brush-torn from the long walk the young robbers had given him. Sweat poured down his face, leaving trails in the dust that clung there. He looked angry enough to blow apart like a runaway steam boiler.

Innocently Frio said, "I don't know what you're talkin' about. I paid you for those mules."

"And stole back the money!" The fat man cursed wildly in the saltiest border Spanish. He accused Frio of hiring *bandidos* to steal the money that was rightfully El Gordo's and Chapa's.

Understanding came into Tom McCasland's eyes. Quickly he moved the women away. The music had stopped. The people stared.

Florencio Chapa's dark hand dropped to his belt and came up swiftly. A knifeblade flashed. "Gringo!" he hissed. "You are a gringo thief. I will spill your blood like a rooster in the pit!"

Frio pushed away from the table, into the clear. He carried no gun, no knife. He crouched, waiting to try to avoid the bandit's vengeful rush. His lips went dry, for already he could almost feel the cold steel of the blade. Chapa would be too much for a man with bare hands.

Tom McCasland stepped in front of Chapa. "Florencio, he is a friend of mine. He is no thief."

"Out of the way! You are just another gringo now!"

"He has stolen no money. He has been with me." It was a lie, but for a moment Chapa hesitated. Tom went on, his voice holding even. "My government has given you money and guns to fight with. Do you want that to stop?"

It gave Chapa pause. His black eyes still seethed with anger, but reason seemed to be struggling for the upper hand.

"Forget it, Florencio," Tom said. "There will be other days, other rides across the river."

Chapa still hesitated. Then the man in the bright uniform stepped forward. No policeman would have dared interfere with Florencio Chapa, but this man had no fear of him. Juan Cortina said in swift, quiet Spanish, "Go, Florencio my friend. Do not spoil the people's *fandango*."

Chapa glanced at Cortina, his eyes rebellious a moment, then acquiescing. He straightened. Not wanting to, he slowly shoved the knife back into the scabbard at his belt. His sharp eyes fastened again on Frio, and they spoke silently of death. At length he turned on his heel. "Come, brother-in-law," he spoke to El Gordo. "We leave this place."

"But the money. . . ."

"Come. I say we leave."

Chapa took three paces and stopped to turn once more toward Frio, his face deadly. "Gringo, I will see you again!"

It was minute or two before Frio walked back toward Tom and the women. "Thanks, Tom," he said tightly.

He looked at the ashen-faced Amelia McCasland. "I oughtn't to've brought you."

Tears glistened in her eyes. She didn't reply.

Tom said with admiration, "So you skinned them at their own game and got your money back."

"I didn't say that."

"You didn't have to." Concerned, Tom said, "Up to now you've just been another damned gringo to Chapa. From now on you'll be a prime target. You've made an enemy of him, Frio."

Frio said, "I never wanted him for a friend." He turned to the girl. "Amelia, I better take you home."

The music had started again. Slowly the crowd drifted back to its dance, to its monte. Tom saw Cortina still watching him, and he nodded unspoken thanks to the man.

Amelia said shakenly, "Yes, Frio, take me home."

As Frio and Amelia walked away, Luisa Valdez moved up and put her arm in Tom's. She stared gravely after the departing couple. "He is a determined man, Tom. He will fight so long as there is breath in him."

Tom nodded soberly. "I reckon he will."

"If you meet him on the other side of the river, you will have to fight him."

"Luisa, I'm servin' my country. I do what has to be done."

"In the end, one of you may have to kill the other."

Tom drew his lips against his teeth and closed his eyes a moment. "As your people say, Fortune and Death come from above. What can a man do to change Fate?" He took her hand and squeezed tightly and felt the responding pressure of her fingers. "Come, Luisa, let's go home."

5

FRIO WHEELER SQUINTED BACK through the dust at his lumbering wagon train, moving along the brush-edged trail behind him, making poor time because heavy sand tugged stubbornly at the iron-rimmed wheels. The mules strained in harness, sweat shining against their brown hides. They needed a rest, but it was less than a mile now to the well. They could have a rest there, and water too, unless this well had gone dry like some of the others.

Fall had come, but still there had been no effective rain. Where normally his mules could find cured grass, there was only the sand. Along trailside, dust churned by thousands of wagon and cart wheels had settled on the brush with the appearance of a dirty snow. No rain had come to wash it away. Now it was November, and it seemed that half his cargo was Indian corn, carried along of necessity to feed the mules.

Through the dust he saw Happy Jack Fleet coming forward in a trot. Happy wasn't hurrying, so whatever he had on his mind must not be particularly important. Eyes on the trail ahead, Frio stopped and waited. Happy Jack reined up and let his horse blow. Frio smiled at the sight of the young man's eyes, staring from a dust-masked face like two small pools of water in the midst of a desert.

"Must be nice to be an owner," the cowboy said. "Get to ride up front in the clean air instead of back in the dusty drags."

Frio shrugged, still smiling. "But think of the responsibility. Anything happens to these wagons, the loss is all mine. You've got nothin' to lose but your life, and maybe that horse."

"I hadn't thought of it thataway," Happy Jack admitted, his eyes shining with humor. "Guess you do take all the risk." He reached in his pocket and brought out a Havana cigar, bought in Matamoros. He allowed himself just one a day so they would last the whole trip. He wouldn't smoke it. He would simply start chewing on it and eventually wear it away to a nub. "Some of them mules are might' near dried out. Reckon that next well has still got water in it?"

"It had better have," Frio said. "We've about emptied our barrels."

They had counted on the last well they'd passed, for it had contained water when they were on their way north. Now, on the return trip to Brownsville, they had found it dry. They had rationed water from half-empty barrels in hopes that the next one, at least, would still yield. Most of the natural waterholes had dried up or had receded to small stinking bogs rimmed with parched remnants of rank weeds and with the skeletons of starved cattle and wild animals of the brush.

Frio said, "Better ease on back and take up the rear guard again. No better place for *renegados* to hit a train than just before it gets to water. Stock is dry and slow, and the men have got their minds on a drink."

Happy Jack nodded. "Hear of any new raids lately?"

"Army courier the other day told me renegades hit a couple of small wagon trains a little ways south of here. Killed three teamsters, made off with some rifles and war goods. That's why I'm not lettin' my wagons split up, ever again. As many as we are, we can give them a pretty good scrap."

He hadn't seen anything of Tom McCasland since that night at the *fandango*. He had seen Florencio Chapa once, over his rifle sight. Chapa had made an exploratory probe against Frio's wagons but had retired quickly upon finding how much firepower Frio's men could mass against him. He had not tried again, although occasionally Frio felt eyes watching him from the brush.

Chapa hadn't forgotten him. He never would.

Frio slipped his saddlegun out of the boot and took a position in front of the train. Presently he reached the clearing that marked the well. He eased into it with the wariness of a deer edging into an open field to graze. He stopped a moment, spotted the two men at the well—only two—and decided the way was clear. He rode ahead, putting the rifle back into the boot.

A Mexican family had settled here originally, and the ruins of their brush *jacal* had stood until one day last winter when a freighter had accidentally burned the place trying to keep warm. The Mexicans' laboriously hand-dug well was still as good as the first day they had dropped a bucket into it and had drawn up fresh water. That it had a slight salt tang was of little importance. Most water in this country did.

Frio frowned as he recognized the big man at the well—the cotton trader Trammell, who had tried once to hire Frio's wagons. Frio didn't know the tall, heavy-shouldered man beside Trammell, but he thought he could recognize the type. This was one of the kind who always came in troubled times—a tough, a saloon brawler more than likely. He wore a pistol in his waistband and gripped a rifle in his huge, speckled hands. The two men stepped forward as Frio approached. Frio dismounted.

"Howdy, Trammell," he said, his voice flat. "Where did you come from?"

"There's lots of trails through the brush, Wheeler, but they all lead to water. I'm headin' to Matamoros, same as you."

The trader was dirty and unshaven from long days on the trail. He jerked his head toward his companion. "This here is Bouncer Bush. I reckon you've heard of him?"

Frio had, and the name simply confirmed his earlier opinion.

"I got wagons comin'," he said, turning to point his chin at the first of them moving into the clearing. "If you'll pardon me, I'll be drawin' up water for my mules."

Trammell shook his head. "No, you won't."

Frio stiffened. "And why not?"

"Because there's just so much water in that well, and it takes a right smart of time for it to seep more in again. I got some wagons comin' too. I claim first right to that water."

"Your wagons aren't here yet. Mine are."

"But *I'm* here, and so is Bouncer. We rode ahead to stake us a claim. Now you just circle up your wagons and wait, Wheeler. Maybe by noontime we'll be through here."

Frio said, "I got thirsty mules, and they're goin' to have water."

Bush swung the muzzle of his rifle around. Frio looked down its barrel and felt his stomach draw up. "Trammell, you got no right to do this. It's first come, first served on this trail."

"And I was the first come."

"But not with wagons."

"I got Bush here, and he's got a rifle. You got any law that'll countermand that sort of combination?" The cotton trader grinned with sarcasm. "You talked a mite rough to me one time, Wheeler. I been hopin' ever since that I'd get a chance to rub your nose in it a little."

Frio's cheeks blazed with anger. "I never said anything to you that wasn't the truth. This just goes to prove it."

A movement caught Frio's eye. At the edge of the clearing, behind Trammell and Bush, he saw Happy Jack Fleet swing down from his horse. Rifle in hand, the cowboy began moving cautiously forward, trying to make no sound. Frio decided to keep Trammell interested and prevent him from noticing Happy.

"How does it feel to be gettin' rich off other men's blood, Trammell?" Frio asked. "Do you ever wake up at night and think about the boys who are dead because the cotton money that was supposed to buy them guns and ammunition went into your pockets instead?"

Trammell flared. "If it wasn't me, it would be somebody else. It had just as well be me."

"You don't ever worry about those boys up there fightin' the war?"

"Sure I worry; I'm a good Southerner. But I'm a businessman too. This war can't last forever, so I'm goin' to make all I can while I can. If them boys are fated to die anyway, nothin' I do is goin' to hurt them or help them. It's all written down up yonder in a Big Book, everything that's goin' to happen to a man, the date and the place. I can't change a word of it. And if I don't take care of myself, nobody else is goin' to."

Frio said, "Reckon you know what they've got written down in that Big Book for you, Trammell? I hope it's somethin' strong enough to fit the crime."

Face darkening, the trader took an angry step forward, then realized he was about to step between Frio and the rifle. He jumped aside with more agility than Frio would have thought he had. "I got a good notion to let Bouncer take care of you, Wheeler. Lord knows you got it comin'."

Frio smiled. "You waited too long. Now I got a man behind you."

Trammell snickered, thinking it was a trick. Then Happy Jack thumbed back the hammer of his rifle with a click that could have been heard halfway across the clearing. Trammell and Bush whirled, their jaws slack with surprise.

Happy Jack grinned, the unlighted cigar in his mouth, tilted upward. "This look about right to you, Frio?"

Frio walked around to peer into Trammell's astonished face. "I'd say you might be aimin' just a shade high, Happy. Bear down to about the fourth button."

"That's a target I couldn't hardly miss."

Bush dropped his rifle. Frio picked it up and let the hammer down easy, then pitched it off to one side. He took the pistol from Bush's waistband and sent it sailing after the rifle. "Now I reckon you men can sit yourselves down and watch us water our mules."

They brought the wagons out into the clearing. Frio's Mexican teamsters began dividing the wagons into two sections and circling them, curving so that the wagon tongues pointed outward. They started unhitching the mules then. Some of the Mexicans came to help Frio and Happy haul up water out of the well and pour it into hollowed-out trees that served as troughs. It would be a slow process, watering all the teams this way. But time meant little to a mule.

Trammell sat glowering. His own train came into sight while Frio's teamsters were watering the last of Frio's mules and filling the barrels on their wagons. By that time the water in the well had declined almost to the limit of the bucket rope's reach. It would take a while to seep full enough again to water Trammell's stock.

"Well, Trammell," Frio said, "we'll hit the trail again directly and turn this over to you. A man ought to've just shot you a while ago and left you here. Try somethin' like that again and maybe I just will."

Contemptuously he turned his back on the cotton trader and swung onto his sorrel horse. He looked a moment at Trammell's wagons filing out of the chaparral. There must have been thirty of them. At up to sixteen bales per wagon, that was not much short of five hundred bales on the one train. No wonder Trammell had been concerned about establishing a claim on the water, even an invalid claim. This much cotton at the present eighty-cents-a-pound river market represented a fortune.

Frio signaled his Mexican *caporal*. "Let's head them out!" He took the lead and moved on down the trail, pointing south. Behind him Happy Jack sat his

horse, watching the wagons move into place and
singing a Confederate war song dedicated irreverently
to Abraham Lincoln:

> "You are a boss, a mighty hoss
> A-snortin' in the stable;
> A racer too, a kangaroo,
> But whip us if you're able!"

Frio saw the dust first, then heard the sound of the
horses. He drew the saddlegun, raising it over his head
in the signal that would stop the train behind him. He
glanced backward and saw the teamsters getting their
wagons ready. Two gun-carrying outriders moved up,
one on either side of the train. At the rear, Happy Jack
came spurring fast. He overtook the outriders and sent
one back to cover the end of the train. He galloped his
horse up and reined him in beside Frio.

"We fixin' to have company?" It was a needless
question, for he could see the dust.

The first riders came into view. Frio stood in the
stirrups, looking through a spyglass he had won from a
ship's officer in a Matamoros monte game. "Soldiers,
Happy."

"Ours?"

"Who else?"

"The way they've stripped the garrison at Fort
Brown, it's been just like sendin' old Abe an engraved
invitation."

"That's the way of war. The privates fight to win it,
and the generals give it away."

Frio recognized the men as some of General Bee's
command out of Fort Brown. The soldiers pulled their
horses to a stop in front of Frio and Happy. One was a
lieutenant.

Happy said, "Say, boys, the river's thataway," pointing in the direction from which the soldiers had come.

"So are the Yankees!" replied the lieutenant excitedly. "We've just abandoned the fort. The Yankees have landed at Brazos Santiago!"

Frio felt as if one of his mules had kicked him in the belly. This was news he had expected for months, yet he wasn't ready for it. He swallowed hard. "You sure about that, lieutenant?"

"There's no question of it, sir. Last spy report we had was that there were nearly thirty transports. Rumor was that ten thousand troops were moving on Brownsville, with Texas renegades from across the river showing them the way."

Frio swore, watching the rest of the Confederate entourage moving up rapidly. His mind went quickly to Amelia McCasland, and Meade. "What about the civilians in Brownsville?"

"Most of the Anglos are getting across the river as quick as they can. When we left they had the ferries jammed with household goods. They were pushing and shoving, fighting for places on board. It was an awful mess."

Anger touched Frio. "And you just rode off and left them that way?"

"Some of us would have stayed and fought, but the general said no. The handful of troops we had left wouldn't have held the Yankees back long." He looked behind him. "You'd better move these wagons aside and leave the trail for the general. He'll probably burn them anyway."

"The hell he will!" Frio blurted.

He turned and signaled for the wagons to move off the road. The signal was unnecessary, for the lieutenant passed the word to every teamster as he rode by. Frio and Happy Jack sat their horses in the trail and waited.

At length the general came, riding on an ambulance. He was forty-one years old, General Hamilton Prioleau Bee, and looked much older. He had been a state legislator from Laredo before the war, and he was destined to become a hero in battle before the war was done. But this was not his heroic day. His face was red with excitement and pressure. His hands were unsteady.

"Whose train is this?" he asked quickly.

"Mine, sir," replied Frio.

The general peered at him with narrowed eyes. "Oh, yes, Wheeler, isn't it? You've already heard? The Yankees are coming."

"I heard."

"I have orders from General Magruder in Austin not to let a bale of cotton fall into enemy hands. We fired all the cotton that was left in Brownsville before we retreated. We'll have to burn yours."

Frio squared himself in the saddle, his mouth turning down at the corners. "Not my cotton. I had *my* orders too. They were to get this cotton to Matamoros. You're not goin' to burn it!"

Bee stiffened at the unexpected disobedience. He started to reply, then sputtered. Frio could see the man's experience in evacuating Brownsville had left him almost totally unstrung. Bee studied a moment, then said, "Very well, not all of the cotton then. Dump half of it and set it afire. Maybe with only half a load you can keep these wagons moving at a good pace northward. We'll rally at King's Ranch and work out a plan of action."

Frio shook his head. "I've already worked out mine. I'm hangin' onto this cotton. Burn the other trains if you can, but you're leavin' mine alone!"

Bee sputtered again. "I've given you an order, sir!"

"I'm not a soldier." Frio leaned forward in the saddle. His voice dropped almost to a whisper, but it had the sting of a whip. "If you fire this cotton, you'll have to kill me first!"

Bee's mouth dropped open, but no sound came. He glanced around him to see if he had the support of his troops. He did.

Frio said, "General, the South needs this cotton. One way or another, I'm goin' to try to get it across the river. But I promise you this: If it ever looks like it's fixin' to be captured, I'll set it afire myself."

The troops pressed in, ready to follow their general's orders even if it meant blasting Frio Wheeler out of the saddle. But General Bee finally shrugged. He was angry, yet he was impressed by the unyielding freighter who sat here and defied him in the face of impossible odds.

"Very well, Wheeler. On that promise, I'll leave you your wagons. God help you." He thought a moment, then added, "God help us all!"

A moment later he was gone in a cloud of dust, trailed by mounted troops and by some forty wagons and carts carrying what supplies he had been able to salvage before putting the fort and the cottonyard to the torch.

When they had gone, Frio sat his horse in the middle of the trail, watching the dust slowly settle. His shoulders sagged, for the weight of the news bore heavily upon him. He seethed with anxiety for the McCaslands. He wanted to forget about the wagons and rush into Brownsville to find out what had happened to Amelia and Meade. But he knew his first responsibility was here. With the world collapsing around him, he had to save this cotton, had to get it across the river for the Confederacy.

Still, a man couldn't just rush blindly ahead.

Happy Jack sat quietly awhile, waiting. Finally, impatient, he asked, "Well, what next, Frio? What're we goin' to do?"

Frio shook his head, not answering.

Happy said, "This sure does clabber the sweetmilk. I been lookin' ahead real hard to some fun in Matamoros. Last time I was there I found a place that had a real pretty little dancin' girl. I swear, Frio, she was barefooted clear up to her chin."

Frio growled, "Hush, Happy, and let me think." In a moment he said, "I'm sorry, I didn't go to be so ornery. It's just that...." His face twisted, and he broke off. But a minute later he straightened in the saddle. "Let's get these wagons out into the chaparral, Happy. Get them plumb out of sight from the road. Later on, you come back with some of the men and brush out the tracks. We don't want anybody to find that cotton."

"And you, Frio? What're you goin' to do?"

"I'm goin' to Brownsville. I've got to scout around and see what's happened. If I'm not back here by this time tomorrow, fire the cotton and head north. You're on your own."

"Them Yankees will nail your hide to the fence." There was no levity in Happy's face now. "I'll go with you."

"No. You stay and see that the job is done right." He touched spurs to the sorrel and said, *"Adiós."*

A little later he turned once and saw white smoke

rising from somewhere to the north. Trammell's wagon train, he knew. Bee had reached the well, and he hadn't listened to Trammell as he had listened to Frio.

There goes Trammell's fortune, Frio thought, and he had not a spark of sympathy for the trader.

6

THE SOUTH WIND BROUGHT him the stench of smoke long before he reached the town. Dusk closed in. Through it he could see flames lick upward and drop again. Some of Brownsville was still burning. On his way in he had met refugees running north. Most of them could give him little information. No, they hadn't seen the Yankees yet, but they were coming.

There were more than twenty thousand troops, one panic-stricken old woman told him, half shrieking. They had been taken out of the Eastern jails and insane asylums just for this job. Their officers had given them whisky to make them mad drunk, and now they were coming to slaughter the town.

Darkness caught him, and he knew he was lucky that it did. It would be a foolhardy stunt to ride into Brownsville in daylight, not knowing the whereabouts of the Union troops, not knowing the situation in the town. He could see a steady glow, probably from the cotton bales slowly burning away on the riverbank. Now and again, a fresh blaze sprang up. Occasionally he caught the sound of gunfire.

If the Yankees were there, someone had remained to show them resistance.

For the first time, a half-panicky thought struck him. What if it were not Yankees? What if the troops had not yet arrived? With the town wide open, defenseless, it would be like a magnet to all the motley border rabble from both sides of the river. It would give them an opportunity to pillage and burn with impunity, for there would be no law, no retribution.

A fresh anxiety welled up in him. If Amelia was still there. . . .

He spurred into a lope.

At the first *jacales* he met a Mexican coming out from the direction of town. The Mexican turned off the trail and started to run.

"Don't be afraid," Frio called to him in Spanish. "I won't hurt you."

The Mexican came up uncertainly, ready to run at the first sign of treachery. Frio asked, "Have the Yankee troops arrived in Brownsville yet?"

Sombrero in hand, the man replied, "No, señor, no *yanquis*. But there are many *bandidos*. It is dangerous to go into the town now."

"What of the people?"

"Many have gone across the river." His eyes rolled upward as he remembered. "Aiii, what a terrible sight, all the fires, all the people screaming. . . ."

He told Frio how General Bee had dropped his siege guns into the river, how he had set fire to the fort and the supplies he had not been able to move. Despairing of getting all the Confederate cotton across the river,

Bee had ordered his men to set ablaze all of it that remained on the north bank. Finally Bee and his troops had started out hurriedly to overtake their wagon train and put the abandoned town far behind them.

The Mexican told of frightened townspeople struggling to get their most valuable possessions onto the ferries and flee across the river. There were so many that ferries and skiffs could not hope to carry them all. Desperate men paid exorbitant prices and still fought with fists and clubs to win places on the boats for themselves, their families, and their belongings. Household and store goods were piled high along the bank of the river. Fires from Fort Brown began to spread out into the town, setting the frame buildings ablaze. Finally the flames had touched a huge cache of gunpowder in the fort. The concussion knocked people to the ground, caved in the sides of nearby buildings, and hurled blazing debris high into the air. Some of it came down amid the piled goods awaiting the ferries, and the riverbank became a heartbreaking holocaust. Many a family lost everything they owned.

The Mexican trembled as he told of the things he had seen. "Some of the people stayed on this side of the river, and now the outlaws have come to steal what has not burned. Bad men, señor—Mexicans, gringos, men with no country. More people will die tonight."

A tingling played up and down Frio's back. He started to touch spurs to the sorrel. The Mexican said, "Do not go. It is not safe there."

"Is it safe anywhere?" Frio asked him. He put the sorrel into a lope. As he rode, he drew the saddlegun and gripped it in his right hand, ready. Moving down Elizabeth Street he came into the heavy dry smell of smoke. It pinched his nostrils, burned his eyes. He coughed, gasping for fresh air. A gust of clean wind came from the south, clearing his lungs.

The fires had not touched the upper end of the street. He could see looters at work in abandoned stores, frantically pulling goods down from the shelves, searching out the things they wanted. He heard someone challenge a pair of men who came out of a store, their arms loaded. The two dropped their loot and attacked the man who had spoken to them. They beat him to his knees with their gun barrels. Frio rode in and fired the rifle once in their direction. The two men broke into a run, disappearing down a dark alley. One of them paused a moment to snap off a wild shot that missed Frio by a considerable distance. The slug struck a brick building across the street and whined away. The beaten man staggered inside the store.

Keeping to the shadows, Frio put the sorrel into a long trot down the street toward the McCaslands'. As he rode, his anxiety swelled and grew. The farther he went, the brighter danced the flames ahead of him. Much of that part of town nearest the fort was either ablaze or already burned. The stench was heavy. His lungs ached from breathing the smoke.

Every few moments he heard a vagrant shot, or two or three. Somewhere, here and there, people were defending their homes, their stores.

He reached the McCasland block. His smoke-burned eyes peered through the eerie firelight for the store with the high false front, the empty balcony that Meade McCasland had disliked so much. He saw it, and his heart leaped. It was ablaze. From out in the street, three men knelt and fired into the flames. Inside, someone fired back.

Frio shifted the rifle to his left hand, with the reins, and drew his six-shooter. He spurred the sorrel into a hard run and headed straight for the three men, firing as he rode. For a moment they held steady and returned his fire. Then one of them slumped. The other two grabbed him and pulled him into the darkness of an alley. Frio fired after them until he realized he was wasting his ammunition. He might need it before he was through here.

The sorrel was dancing wildly at sight of the flames. Frio jumped to the ground beside a dropped bundle of clothes he saw in the street. He picked a shirt from among the garments and tied it across the horse's eyes, blinding him.

"Amelia!" he called. "Meade!" Over the crackle of the flames he heard no response. "Amelia!" he called again.

From inside the blazing store he heard her answer. "Frio! Frio!"

He moved the horse along the side of the building where the flames had not yet reached. He tied the blindfolded animal across the street and then tried the door. It was bolted from inside. On the ground he saw an empty wooden packing crate. Using this, he smashed a window and crawled inside. He found himself in the living quarters.

"Amelia!"

He heard her answer from up front, in the store. She was locked in. He twisted his body and struck the dividing door with his shoulder. The latch section splintered, and the door fell open. The blistering heat slapped him across the face.

He saw her framed amid the crackling flames. She was sobbing aloud as she tried vainly to pull a man's body across the floor ahead of the rapidly gaining fire. The boy Chico huddled in a corner, eyes wide in fear.

The fallen man was Meade McCasland, and Frio

could tell he was hard hit. But there was no time to think of that. There might not even be time to get him out of the building before the blazing ceiling came crashing down upon them. Frio grabbed Meade from behind and half lifted him up, dragging the old man's heels as he hurriedly started backing out.

"Get out, Amelia, Chico! Out the door, quick!"

Chico unfroze and bolted out the door Frio had smashed. Amelia hung back, her hands cupped almost at her mouth, her eyes swimming in tears.

Frio got Meade McCasland through the door. A moment later the ceiling caved in. Now the living quarters were beginning to burn. "We've got to get clear," Frio cried. "We've got to get to the street."

Amelia hurried ahead of him and unbolted the back door. The furnace heat seared Frio's lungs as he knelt and worked Meade's limp body up over his back so he could walk upright and carry the wounded man. Frio went out first, pistol in his hand. The girl and the little boy followed him. Across the street, where Frio had tied the sorrel, the flames had not yet reached. Bent over by Meade's weight, Frio struggled across and gently laid the man down on a porch. Then, in the crazy dancing light of the blaze, he knelt to examine Meade's wound. He found his hands sticky with the old man's blood. Frio tore open Meade's shirt.

Just then Meade gasped and went limp. Frio lifted a wrist and felt for the pulse. There was none. Slowly, gently, he folded the old storekeeper's arms. He turned back to Amelia.

"I'm sorry," he said.

Her hands went over her face, and her shoulders trembled. Frio stood up and took her into his arms. The little boy knelt beside the old man and sobbed brokenly. Across the street the flames swept through the rest of the building. The roof seemed for a moment to buckle, then it went down with a roar that sent sparks high into the air. The sorrel danced in fear, for he could hear and smell even if he could not see.

From down the street, Frio heard a man's voice calling: "Dad! Amelia!" He heard a horse running, and he saw the figure break into sight. The man slid the horse to a stop and for a moment appeared on the verge of rushing into the blazing hull of McCasland's store.

"Dad!" he called again. "Amelia!"

Frio shouted, "Over here, Tom!"

Tom McCasland came running, leading the horse. He let the horse go, and it went to Frio's sorrel. Tom grabbed Amelia. "Amelia, are you all right?"

Then his gaze dropped to the floor of the porch. He choked, "Dad!" and knelt quickly. He touched the hands and knew without having to ask. His body trembled as he slowly, lovingly moved his fingers over the quiet, still face. Finally he asked, "How did it happen?"

Frio said, "Looters. I just got here myself."

Amelia McCasland forced herself to speak. Her voice was thin. "Dad wouldn't leave. Said this was his home. Said he hadn't ever run in his life. He didn't think the Yankees would hurt us. He didn't count on this." She looked across the street at the death throes of the building that had been home. She cried a moment, then controlled herself. "With dark, the looters came. He tried to run them off with a rifle. They threw a lighted lantern through the window, then shot him as he tried to beat out the flames."

Tom choked. "If I had known . . . If I had had any idea . . . I was out at Brazos Santiago, where the troops were landing. I thought sure you-all would cross to Matamoros before the trouble started."

Frio said, "Where are the Yankees at, Tom? Have they got here yet?"

Tom shook his head. "They'll get here, but it'll be a while. There's a storm out on the gulf. They're havin' a hard time gettin' the transports unloaded."

"How many troops?"

"Seven thousand seasick soldiers."

Frio took hold of the girl's arms. "Amelia, we've got to move. I'll take you anywhere you want to go, but we've got to get away from here. Some of those looters will be around again. They'd better not catch a woman out in the street."

She nodded woodenly and knelt to look at her father again. "What about Dad?"

Frio said, "I reckon we'll have to leave him to Tom."

Tom said, "Yes, Frio, I'll take care of Dad. But you're not goin' anyplace."

Frio turned quickly and found Tom McCasland holding a pistol on him. "Tom, what is this?"

"I'm placin' you under arrest, Frio. I'm goin' to hold you till the Union troops get here."

Frio swayed. He would have expected almost anything but this. "Tom, we've been friends for so long . . . ."

"That's why I'm doin' it. Leave you free to ride up and down in the chaparral and somebody'll kill you sure. Because you *are* my friend, Frio, I want to see you live. I want to put you away in some safe Union prison camp till this war is over. I want to see you stay alive to marry my sister and be the father of her children."

Frio's voice held an edge of steel. "Do this, Tom, and you'll never be my friend again."

"I've got no choice. I want you to live, even if you hate me for it. Now ease that pistol out of the holster and drop it."

"You wouldn't really kill me."

"But I'd wound you. I'd cripple you if it meant keepin' you alive. Drop the pistol, Frio."

Frio dropped the pistol. It clattered on the porch. Amelia McCasland stared at it a moment. Then she picked it up. She swung it around to point at her brother.

"Now, Tom, you drop yours."

"Sis!"

"Drop it, I said."

Stubbornly Tom held his ground. "What're you doin' this for, Sis? I'm only tryin' to help you and Frio."

"Whatever Frio wants, that's what I want. If he wants to be free ... if he wants to keep fighting ... then that's what I want for him. Drop the gun."

"You're my sister. You wouldn't kill me."

"Like you told Frio, I'd wound you. I'd cripple you if I had to."

Her voice was rock steady. She meant it, and Tom knew she did. He shifted the pistol around in his hand and gave it to Frio butt first. "You're makin' a mistake, Frio. This was a way out for you if you'd just taken it."

Frio said, "The war's not over yet, Tom. As long as it's still on, I'll do my part as I see it." He jerked his head toward the two horses. "I reckon we'll have to take your horse."

Grudgingly Tom said, "Help yourself. There's nothin' I can do."

Frio and Amelia moved toward the horses. Amelia wore a housedress with long skirts that were going to make it difficult for her to ride astride. "Can you manage?" he asked her.

She nodded. "I'll have to."

He gave her a footlift onto Tom's horse and looked away as she pulled the skirts up. When she was in the saddle, he turned to his sorrel. He pulled away the blindfold and mounted. "Come along, Chico," he said to the little boy and swung him up behind the saddle. Chico's arms went around Frio's waist, taking a death grip.

Amelia had a last look at the gutted store and at her father lying on the porch, his one remaining son standing with shoulders slumped in sorrow. Tightly she said, "Take me out of here, Frio."

They moved away from the flames, away from the terror that was Brownsville on this, the blackest of its nights.

7

WATER WAS ALWAYS THE first consideration of
those adventuresome men who turned to cattle-raising
in antebellum Texas. They could find grass almost
anywhere—free grass—but water was often a rare
commodity. The early Mexican rancheros in lower
Texas settled wherever they located living water, or
where they could dig shallow wells and find a depend-
able supply. If grass ran out, cattle could still survive
for a time on dried mesquite beans and the many kinds
of brush. If water played out, death was as certain as a
change in the moon.

Frio Wheeler and Tom McCasland had bought their
land from crusty old Salcido Mendoza, who had
fought against Zachary Taylor in the Mexican War.
Media Mejico—half Mexico—the natives called the
region between the Nueces and the Rio Grande. Mendoza could see to his disgust that it was inevitably

becoming gringo country. He didn't want to live here
anymore and be forced to rub shoulders with con-
tentious, pale-eyed adventurers from the north, not
when he could move south of the Rio and find land
that would remain forever *puro Mejicano*.

A warm feeling always came to Frio when he rode
out of the brush and gazed upon this headquarters,
scattered without plan or form below the never-failing
spring. The improvements weren't much to look at,
but they belonged to him: Mendoza's old rock house
that was Frio's living quarters—the few times he was
ever able to sleep there anymore; the smaller stone
house in which Blas and María Talamantes lived; the
shady brush arbors, the several brush *jacales* that
Mendoza had built for his help, all of them empty
now because war had left the ranch without labor; the
far-flung brush corrals, built—like everything else
here—of materials that the land itself had yielded up.

When Frio and Tom had come to their last violent quarrel over the war and had broken their partner-
ship, they had split their holdings down the middle.
They had drawn for high card, and Frio had won this
headquarters.

Frio had had little time for sleep since the burning
of Brownsville. Shoulders sagging in weariness, his
face grimy and bearded, he turned in the saddle and
looked back at his jolting wagons, trailing along far
behind him. The mules were dry and tired but still
straining against the harness. Dust hit the rear wagons.
Amelia McCasland rode on the one in lead, beside a
leather-skinned teamster. She sat hunched, numb from
grief, near exhaustion. Her face seemed to have
thinned. The weather had turned cold, and blue fingers
held a blanket around her shoulders.

As the wagons came up even with him, Frio said, "We're here, Amelia."

She straightened. A little of the dullness left her eyes. She looked a long time and said, "It's the prettiest sight I ever saw."

She had visited here many times when Frio and Tom had been partners. Those had been warm and glowing days, a time for youthful dreams, for songs and happy laughter. Seemed there was precious little chance for happiness anymore.

Down the creek, longhorn cattle caught sight of the wagons emerging from the brush. They hoisted their tails and clattered off into the thickets, leaving only dust to show where they had been. These *cimarrones* were outlaw cattle that had lost domesticity in the centuries since their ancestors had escaped from Coronado and others of the early Spaniards. Of all colors and fleet as deer, they had reverted to a primal state almost as wild as the wolves and the panthers. It took fast horses to overtake them, strong men to bring them to hand. Frio had gloried in that kind of work during his free years before the war. Many a time he had camped around a waterhole with Blas and Tom McCasland, waiting to catch these wild cattle as they came up to drink. It was an adventure that lifted men's spirits, though it broke their bones and tore their hides.

Blas Talamantes left the ranch outbuildings and rose toward the wagons, a rifle ready across his lap. Recognizing Frio, he spurred into a lope.

"Frio," he said in astonishment, looking at the wagons. "What for you come here with the cotton?"

"Had to go someplace. The Yankees took Brownsville."

Blas slumped in the saddle, regret in his eyes. He

saw Amelia McCasland on the lead wagon, and his gaze cut back to Frio with a question. Frio said, "They killed her father and burned his place. I couldn't leave her there."

"*Así es la suerte,*" Blas murmured, accepting tragedy as a fact of life. "Bad luck. María has our house warm. We take her there."

Frio nodded tiredly. "Fine. We got a boy with us, too."

The boy Chico sat huddled on the second wagon, bundled in a blanket. Nothing showed but his eyes and his nose.

"If he is a boy," said Blas, "he will be hungry. María will fix something."

They led the wagons down to the house and into the open gate of one of the big brush corrals. While the teamsters and Happy Jack Fleet began unhitching the mules, Frio helped Amelia down from the wagon. She shivered from the chill and rewrapped the blanket around her. Blas Talamantes reached up for the boy and carried him in his arms, talking softly to him in Spanish.

María Talamantes stood in the open door of her stone house, watching with wide and puzzled eyes. "*Entre,*" she spoke to Frio and the girl.

Frio said, "María, this is Amelia. She'll be here awhile."

María bowed. She was a tiny woman, not more than five feet tall. "*Mucho gusto de verle.*" Blas gently set the boy down upon the hard-packed dirt floor. Chico's blanket dropped, and his bewildered, cold-purpled face lifted toward María. He seemed about ready to cry, for tragedy and change had come too rapidly for him to grasp. María exclaimed, "*Pobrecito,*" and knelt to feel his stiffened hands. "Poor boy. Come to the fire. We will get you something warm to eay *muy pronto*."

Amelia and the little boy warmed themselves by the open fireplace, where blackened pots were hanging to heat over the crackling flames. "We have beans and chili," María said. "I will fix coffee too. It is good weather for hot food."

The bright-eyed little woman got busy putting coffee on to boil, setting bowls on the small table. She was a good cook, if a man's taste ran toward Mexican foods, and Frio's did. He had often thought the best thing that had happened to this place was Blas's marrying her and bringing her here from Matamoros. Since María's arrival, Frio had never had to eat his own cooking when he was at the ranch.

Frio noticed the telltale swelling of her stomach. He glanced at Blas. "You didn't tell me. Which is it goin' to be, a boy or a girl?"

Blas smiled with pride. "A boy, for sure. All the Talamantes children were boys."

"*Ojalá,*" Frio said. "For you, I hope so."

María did not slow down until she had all the food on the table, and she sat then only because Amelia insisted upon it. Mexican women took pregnancy as a natural condition and did not coddle themselves because of it. A young married woman was usually in one stage or another of pregnancy.

Frio ate silently. Finished, he said to María and Blas, "The señorita will be here awhile, she and the boy. They've had a bad run of luck." Briefly he told what had happened. He watched Amelia's face tighten and feared she might cry. But she remained dry eyed. It came to him then that she was probably tougher than he had given her credit for.

María stared gravely at the girl, her black eyes soft with sympathy. "Have no worry, Frio. We will take good care of her."

Later Frio walked over to his own house, carrying with him coals from María's fire. He put them into his cold fireplace and with his big Bowie knife began to peel shavings from dry wood to work up a blaze. Presently he had a good fire going.

Hearing someone enter, he turned. Amelia pushed the door shut behind her and stood with the blanket draped over her shoulders. She said nothing.

Frio remarked, "Coaxin' up a fire to take the chill off the place. You can have this house, Amelia, for as long as you want it."

She slid the blanket off her shoulders and dropped it onto a chair. "What will you do?"

"Go on with the wagons, try to get them across the river somehow."

"When will you be back?"

He shrugged. "*Quién sabe?* War like it is, who can tell?"

Her hair was in pleasant disorder about her cold-flushed face, and he could see beauty there, even with the tragedy in her eyes. She moved closer. "Don't leave too soon. Your men need rest. *You* need rest."

"The war won't stand still."

She put her arms around him and leaned her head against his chest. "I don't want you to leave me, Frio, not yet. I want you to stay here with me, just a little while." Her arms tightened. "Just stay and hold me, and don't let go."

Standing with arms tight about her, he buried his face in her sweet-smelling hair. He held her silently and listened to the crackling of the fire.

* * *

Frio loped well ahead of the wagons and reined the sorrel down toward the river. He pulled in at a mud-plastered *jacal* a hundred yards back from the bank. An old Mexican stuck his head distrustfully around the side of the hut. Slowly recognizing Frio beneath the dust and the whiskers, he stepped out into the open, smiling broadly. He hunched his shoulders, which were covered by a faded old serape so worn that it looked as if rats had been chewing away the edges.

"My friend the Frio," he said, pleased. "A good name for this kind of weather, for it is a little *frio*, a little cold."

"*Qué tal?*" Stepping to the ground, Frio took the old man's hand. In Spanish he said, "Good to see you, Don Andres. It has been too long. One does not have time these days to visit friends."

The gray-bearded man shook his head. "Too much of the war. It seems there is always time for war, but never enough time for one's friends. Come inside. Perhaps I can find something fit for a friend to drink."

The old man lived alone in the hut, for his wife was buried in a tiny picket-fenced enclosure a little way upriver. Most of his children had scattered to the winds, only a couple of them still living nearby. The tiny house was a boar's nest. A bright-feathered game-cock sat with all the pride of ownership on the edge of the old man's unmade cot, secured by a leather thong tied to its leg. Don Andres patted the fighting rooster as he walked by.

"It could be worse, Frio," he said. "We could be like the rooster and have only enemies."

From a shelf Don Andres took a clay jug and handed it to Frio. "The first drink is for my good friend."

Frio took a swallow and choked. He passed the jug

back to the old man. "If that is what you give your friends, what do you give your enemies?"

"I have no enemies. Living far out here on the river, I cannot afford them." He took a long drink and shook his head. "The pulque is not as good as it used to be. Nothing is as good as it used to be. The young ones, they have lost the touch." He drank three long swallows and wiped his mouth with the gnarled knuckles of his left hand. "I am glad that I am old and am not much longer for this world. All grace and beauty has left it. And all the good pulque."

He sat down at a tiny table and beckoned for Frio to take one of the rickety rawhide chairs. He set the jug on the table between them. "Did you come to visit an old man, or is it war business that brings you here?"

"I must admit, old friend, that I am here of necessity. You know that the Yankee troops have taken Brownsville?"

The *viejo* nodded gravely. "Do not let it concern you, Frio. In my life I have seen many armies come across this land. Always they go again. One has only to wait and be patient."

"I have all my wagons with me, Don Andres. I have no time for patience."

The old man thoughtfully rubbed his bearded chin. "The young ones never do. How can I help?"

"For one thing, I need information. Have you seen any bluecoat troops come this way?"

Don Andres nodded. "A *yanqui* patrol came yesterday. It was on its way upriver."

Frio frowned. "You have no idea how long it might be before it passes this way again?"

"I asked no questions. I thought if they wished me to know anything, they would tell me without my having to ask. And they told me nothing."

Frio clenched his fist, helplessness rousing an anger in him. "They might not come back for days, or they might be here in an hour."

"If I had even dreamed you would wish to know. . . ."

Frio waved his hand, dismissing the subject. "Do you still run your ferry?"

Don Andres nodded. "*Sí*. It is old and broken down like myself. But, blessed be God, it is still there, and somehow it still finds its way across the river." His eyebrows went up. "You would cross your wagons on Andres's little ferry?"

"I have no choice. Either I cross them here or I have to take them all the way upriver to Laredo, perhaps even to Eagle Pass. I am too close to the river for that now. The Yankees would find me."

"Perhaps they may find you anyway. It will take a long time to cross your wagons with my little wreck of a ferry."

"It's the only one there is. We'll rush it."

Old Don Andres took another long swallow from the jug. "Once I was young and always in a hurry. But I finally learned that one does not rush the river, Frio. If one takes it on its own terms and at its own pace, he lives to be an old man like me. If he does not, then he dies, and the river goes on without him."

He extended the jug to Frio, but Frio shook his head, too preoccupied to care about a drink. Don Andres placed the jug back on its shelf and stretched himself. "But we shall see how much we can hurry it. Who wants to live forever?"

Blas had come along to help. Frio sent him downriver to look for any sign of patrols. He sent Happy

Jack upriver to hunt the Yankee troops that had been here yesterday.

"Now, boys," he told both of them, "some people claim that any Rebel can whip a dozen Yankees, but I'm afraid they've stretched things a mite. Don't mix it with them none. Just try to slip away without bein' seen and get back here as fast as you can run."

Happy Jack had winked at Blas. "Bet you if the truth was known, a Rebel couldn't whip more than *half* a dozen of them."

Frio had eyed Happy Jack narrowly, not sure but what the young hellion would spark a fight if he thought he had half a chance. "Mind me now, Happy. You get yourself back here if you see any Yankees. And try not to bring them with you."

When the pair had gone their separate ways, Frio signaled the wagons out of the brush and down toward the river. Usually he was happy to leave the closeness of the chaparral and break out into the open. This time he felt somehow naked and helpless without the mesquite and the "wait-a-minute" catclaw to help hide his cargo of cotton.

He rode on down to the river, where Don Andres waited at the ferry with a pair of his grandsons who were to help. Frio swung down for a critical look at the ancient conveyance. It was one of the old-fashioned kind that used the river's own current for its motive power. A heavy rope strung across the river kept the ferry from being carried away. Frio frowned. Like the *viejo* had said, the ferry had been here a long time. Too long, perhaps. The old lumber had twisted and rotted. Here and there Frio could see holes almost big enough for a man to stick his foot through. But people didn't use the ferry much anymore. Don Andres didn't earn enough from it to justify fixing it up. It kept him in beans and chili and pulque. When he was gone, the ferry probably would go too.

"Not very big, is it, Don Andres?"

The old man shook his head. "When I was a young man and built it, it was for burros, and sometimes for oxcarts. We had nothing bigger in those days. We had never seen anything like your gringo wagons."

Through the years the ferry had been used largely by smugglers, moving goods into Mexico without having to pay a duty such as was required in Matamoros or the other legal crossing points. By rights, the Mexican government should have burned this ferry years ago. But when, every so often, the customs officers came around, Don Andres made it a point always to have some coin hidden away so he could pay them their *mordida*. "Little bite," the word meant in English. It was an unwritten law on the Mexican side of the river, a courtesy payment for services rendered, or for action withheld. The Americans would have called it a bribe, but then, the *yanquis* were notorious for being too blunt. *Mordida* was a much better-sounding word.

Frio stepped off the ferry's length, his mouth going grim. It would hold one loaded wagon at a time. It wouldn't take a team of mules. For one thing, it wasn't big enough. For another, some of them might break their legs stepping through the holes. No, they would have to swim the mules. Low as the river was, there wouldn't be a great deal of swimming to it.

Don Andres was plainly chagrined over the shortcomings of his equipment. He shrugged and said apologetically, "A poor man has only a poor man's ways."

Frio replied, "We'll make the best of it." He signaled for the *caporal* to bring along the first wagon.

The heavy brake dragged in shrill protest against the rear wheels as the wagon started down the incline. Frio climbed the bank to look for any sign of Blas or Happy Jack. He didn't expect to see either one and hoped he wouldn't. If they came back this soon, it could only mean trouble.

They weren't in sight. He returned to the water's edge, where the ferry bobbed gently up and down at its mooring.

"We'll put the team across first," he said to Don Andres and the *caporal*. "Then it can pull each wagon off the ferry and up the other bank."

A couple of teamsters took off most of their clothes and pitched them onto the first wagon, where they would stay dry. Then, shivering with cold, they moved the mule team out into the water and splashed across the river.

Frio and the other teamsters put shoulders to the first wagon and grunted and pushed it onto the ferry, tongue first. Panting hard, Frio stepped back onto the dry ground and waved his hat.

"Take it across, Don Andres."

Frio stood and watched while he tried to regain his breath. The river wasn't particularly wide at this point; the main reason the old ferryman had picked this place to set up long years ago. But right now it seemed to Frio that it must be half a mile to the Mexican side. Old Don Andres and his two young grandsons used long poles to shove the ferry out into the stream. Carefully they quartered it around so that the current began to catch the conveyance and carry it along.

Impatience gnawed at Frio as he watched the ferry's snail-paced movement across the brown Rio. The great weight of the wagon and cargo was almost too much for the ancient conveyance. It pushed the platform so far down that water lapped up over the side. A little imbalance might tip it.

The *caporal* brought down another wagon and moved it into position. Across the river, the two naked and cold teamsters had the mule team waiting when the ferry reached the far side. The first thing they did was put on the dry clothes it had brought along. Then they hitched onto the wagon and pulled it up the south bank, hauling it well out of the way. As the ferry returned, the teamsters unhitched the mules and brought them back to the small mooring for a second wagon.

So it went, one wagon at a time, at an eternally slow pace. Over and over, Frio counted the wagons as each one reached the far bank—three, four, five, six, seven. And still seven on this side, waiting to cross.

He heard a running horse. A Mexican teamster called him and pointed upriver. Frio swung onto his sorrel and moved up the bank. He saw Happy Jack spurring hell-for-leather, horse beginning to lather.

Happy slid to a stop. Arm outstretched, he jabbed a finger toward the northwest. "That bluecoat patrol the old man told you about—it's on its way!"

8

FRIO'S STOMACH DREW INTO a knot. "How far off is it?"

"Five, maybe six miles upriver when I left them. They're just walkin' their horses like they're not too anxious to get back to the fort and go to work."

"Did they see you?"

"If they had, they'd be right behind me. I was careful." His brow furrowed in concern, Happy counted the wagons that still waited on the north bank. "We ain't got time to cross that way, Frio. Them Yankees, they'll be here before you can finish."

Frio frowned, indecisively rubbing the back of his neck. "How many men would you say there were?"

"Twenty-five, maybe thirty." His eyes narrowed. "You ain't about to try and stand them off, are you? Most of these teamsters can't shoot for sour apples. They're no match for them troops."

"No, Happy. I was just thinkin' how we might decoy the federals away for a while, you and me."

"Just us two, and all them Yanks?" Happy Jack stared incredulously. But slowly his mouth began to lift at the corners, and he shrugged. "You're crazy, but I reckon that makes you a match for me. Let's go."

First Frio rode down to speak to the *caporal*. "Unhitch all these teams but one and get some of the boys to swim them across, now. Just leave one team to pull the wagons up to the ferry. When you get the last wagon loaded, swim that team across too. If you see the Yankees comin', set fire to any wagons that are still left on this side. Then get the hell across that river!"

"*Sí, patrón*," the *caporal* said. Before Frio and Happy Jack had ridden away, he was already carrying out the order.

Without talking, Frio and Happy reined their horses northwestward and moved them into an easy lope. They followed the river rail, where Happy had seen the patrol. When they had ridden what Frio estimated to be two and a half or three miles, he pulled northward into the brush. He slowed to a walk and slipped his saddlegun out of the boot.

They heard the patrol before they saw it. The troopers' voices carried sharply through the cold. Frio stood in his stirrups, listening. He turned to Happy. "Ready?"

Happy's lips were drawn tight, and he seemed to be giving the matter some serious second thought. "It's sure an awful lot of Yankees, even for two of us. But I don't aim to let no owner get ahead of me."

"We'll keep our distance," Frio said. "I'm countin' on these Yankees bein' new to the brush country. I expect they'll be mighty cautious. All we need to do is keep them confused long enough to get those wagons across."

Happy admitted, "I'm confused already."

"It's like this: We'll split up a ways, make them think there's several of us. Shoot in their direction once with your rifle, move a little bit and give them a pistol shot or two. I'll do the same. We'll keep movin', that's the main thing. We'll keep drawin' them north, away from the river. And we don't ever want them to get a look at us. Keep them thinkin' we're a bunch."

Happy nodded, dubious but willing. "*Bueno*, you shoot first, when you think it's time. I'll make them think old Rip Ford has brought his whole army back to the Rio Grande."

Frio estimated that he was a hundred and fifty yards north of the trail. Through one half-clear spot in the brush he would be able to glimpse the patrol as it passed. Cold though he was, he felt his hands sweaty against the gunstock. Finally he caught a flash of movement. He raised the rifle to his shoulder and gently brought up the muzzle. He squeezed the trigger, felt the rifle jar against him. His horse jumped, startled, but not before Frio saw a trooper's horse go down.

Frio spurred thirty yards, stopped, and fired again in the direction of the patrol. He heard Happy open up, firing twice, then moving and firing again. Men shouted, and horses began to strike the brush. Frio caught Happy's eye and waved him northward. They spurred away from the river a little farther, then stopped to fire another round of shots.

In confusion, the Yankee patrol commenced a blind, wild shooting into the brush. Frio could hear slugs whine by, snapping against the thin trunks of the winter-dormant mesquites and the catclaw.

Frio and Happy retreated northward again, pulling a little to the west, drawing the patrol away from the river crossing. Only occasionally could Frio catch a glimpse of Union movement. Mostly he had to go by sound. As he had hoped, the federals were proceeding slowly and with caution. This thick South Texas *bosque* was alien to them. Frio and Happy would fire several times, moving between shots, then pull back. The patrol continued to take the bait.

At last Frio signaled Happy to him. "I think we've done what we figured on. We'll go yonderway a little more, then try to sneak east and get back to the ferry while these soldiers are still huntin' around out here."

They rode north a mile. Then, certain they were out of sight and hearing, Frio reined east and spurred into a lope. Happy Jack kept close to him, picking his way through the brush. Happy was grinning in relief.

"It was fun," he said, "but I'm sure glad it's over. Way them Yankees poured lead into that brush, sounded like a bunch of bees. I was afraid somebody might get stung."

They reached the river crossing as the last wagon was pushed onto the bobbing ferry. Frio could see dust on the trail to the north. Whoever was leading that patrol wasn't as slow-witted as Frio had hoped. To the remaining teamsters, Frio said, "You-all get on the ferry and ride across with the wagon. Happy and me, we'll swim the team."

They stripped off their clothes and pitched them onto the ferry. The ferry slid away from the muddy bank. Frio held a moment, watching the dust, trembling from cold.

"Well, Happy," he said, "if we don't want to be shakin' hands with the Yankees, we better take us a swim."

He took up the long lines and led the last team down the bank. Happy brought up the rear, shouting and urging the mules off into the river. Quickly the bottom fell away from beneath the sorrel's feet, and he was swimming. Frio slipped out of the saddle, the cold water almost taking his breath away as it came up over his bare skin. Behind him, Happy went into the water and yelped a little like a coyote. Frio kept hold of the saddlehorn and let the horse carry him along. Behind him splashed the mules. And behind them trailed Happy, holding onto his horse's tail.

The ferry moved slowly along ahead of them, its pace barely enough that the two horsemen and the mule team did not catch up. Finally the ferry drew against its southside mooring, bumping hard. Frio waded up onto dry land, still holding the reins. The teamsters who already had crossed were waiting to grab onto the mules as they drifted out.

Happy dragged himself ashore and turned to look back, trembling with cold.

"We got company over yonder, Frio."

One of the teamsters came running, bringing Frio his dry clothes from the wagon. Shivering, Frio pulled them on while he looked. The Union patrol had stopped at water's edge and stood looking across the river at the quarry it had just missed. One man, afoot, moved in quick, angry strides. Frio guessed him to be the officer in charge. The officer pointed. Half a dozen troopers rode over and cut Don Andres's ferry rope.

Shaking his rough old fist, Don Andres cursed in a manner that he had taken a lifetime to perfect. Some of Frio's teamsters quickly moved to tie the old man's ferry so it would not drift off downriver.

Happy Jack observed, "Sore losers, ain't they?"

Don Andres fumed. "In all the wars that have come

across this land, no one has ever seen fit to cut my rope."

Frio said, "Don't worry, Don Andres. The Confederacy owes you a new one. I'll see that you get it."

The last wagon was drawn up into line with the others. The teamsters had built a large fire, and Frio and Happy Jack went to it to warm themselves. Both were nearly purple from cold.

Well satisfied, Frio said, "Amigos, you've put in a good day's work. We'll camp here and rest. We'll head on down the river toward Matamoros in the mornin'. Nobody's apt to bother us anymore now."

Happy Jack said, "How about them Yankees yonder?"

"They won't cross into Mexico. It was sanctuary to the Yankees and the *renegados* when the Confederacy held the other side. Now it's sanctuary to us."

"They'll follow along with us all the way to Matamoros."

"Let them. They'll learn a lot about handlin' a string of wagons."

"Blas is still over there someplace."

"He'll be all right. When he sees we've made it, he'll slip back to the ranch."

Happy Jack stared awhile at the Yankees, eyes wide in wonderment. These were the first he had ever seen in uniform.

"They don't look no whole lot different from us, do they?"

Frio said in surprise, "Were they supposed to?"

Happy shrugged. "I don't know. Guess I thought they was supposed to have horns and a tail, or somethin'. Outside of the blue coats, they look like us. You couldn't hardly tell no difference."

Frio shook his head. "I don't suppose you could."

Happy Jack held his hands out over the fire and warmed himself, his face creased in thought. "Frio, you reckon we killed any of them with that shootin' we done?"

"We kept a long ways off, and we didn't get much chance to aim. I'd say the chance was mighty small."

Relief came into the cowboy's eyes. "I'm glad. I never killed nobody in my life."

The road followed the river all the way to Matamoros, though it was straighter, sometimes edging southward to avoid duplicating the river's needless bends. As Frio had expected, the patrol followed along all the way. Every time the road came close to water's edge, he could look northward and see the riders on the far side, watching.

As the train entered the western edge of Matamoros, innumerable lanky dogs came bounding forth as a reception committee. Mexican people began to line the streets. Frio could hear people shouting:

"Los algodones vienen!" The cotton men are coming!

Men, women, and children came hurrying to watch this first wagon train with its load of heavy bales. Frio could see in the faces of the adults a considerable measure of relief, even joy. These people had no stake in the gringo war, no particular enthusiasm for either North or South. Many of them actually looked upon the gringo as being akin to the plague, whether he be from Texas or New York. But they had a large stake in the border cotton trade, the hectic commerce the Civil War had brought to Matamoros. Union stoppage of the border trade had threatened ruin to the overgrown Mexican city.

A Matamoros merchant who was a friend of Frio's came trotting out to walk beside Frio's horse and look back down the dusty street at the strung-out wagons. "Then it is not true, Frio, that the *yanqui* troops have stopped the *algodones*?"

Frio shook his head. "Not true, amigo. They've slowed us down, but they won't stop us."

The merchant smiled. "*Bueno.* It had looked like a hungry winter."

Someone shouted, *"Vivan los algodones!"* Others of the crowd took it up, and cheers preceded the wagons down the long, winding street.

Passing a municipal building, Frio glanced up at the second-story iron-grilled balcony, where two men stood looking down upon the wagons. One was a U.S. Army colonel in full dress uniform, evidently here in his finest for a state visit to the powers of Matamoros. Beside him, resplendent in plumes and braid, was the erect figure of Juan Nepomuceno Cortina. Frio could see the Union officer's face flare with wrath and frustration. A half smile crossed the visage of Juan Cortina, for the Mexican could see an ironic humor in this development.

Frio suppressed an urge to give the officer a mock salute. Behind him, Happy Jack had no inhibitions.

"Hey there, Yank," Happy yelled at the colonel, "come on down and I'll let you buy me a drink!"

Frio could see the officer speaking angrily to Cortina and Cortina shrugging as if to say, "What can I do?"

At last Frio reached the riverbank cottonyard the Confederacy had maintained on the Mexican side, opposite Brownsville. He glanced across the muddy waters at the Texas city that now was closed to him. He could still see the charred remains of cotton bales and household goods on the far bank. There was no sign of the riverboats. The Santa Cruz ferry was crossing empty, except for a couple of passengers.

Portly old Hugh Plunkett came hurrying across the nearly empty cottonyard to meet him. "Frio!" he shouted in surprise. "For God's sake, it's Frio!"

Hands outstretched, he reached up and grasped Frio's shoulders and shook the freighter for joy. The cotton agent's eyes glistened with tears as he looked at the wagons trailing in. "Well, I'll swun," he said wonderingly, over and over. "I'll swun." He walked out past the first wagon and stopped, watching the others come in. "How many did you get across with, Frio?"

"All I had. Fourteen."

Plunkett kept shaking his head. "I'll swun. I don't know how you done it. Thought the cotton trade was done for."

"They've crippled us, Hugh, but we're a long way from dead. Before you know it, we'll be bringin' cotton into Matamoros just as heavy as we ever did."

He told the cotton agent how they had done it. "Of course," he said, "nobody else will be able to use Don Andres's old ferry. The Yankees will keep a watch on it. But the Rio Grande is a mighty long river. They can't watch it all the way to Laredo. The cotton trains that are on the road now can swing west and cross way up yonder, beyond the Yankee patrols. It'll add a lot to the trip down from San Antonio—well nigh double it, I expect. But the cotton will come through—that's the main thing."

Plunkett nodded, his eyes glistening as he stared in triumph at the bales Frio had brought in. "Mexican customs officials will be put out about it," he said, "you crossin' where there wasn't a customs house. But a little *mordida* in the right place ought to fix that."

Frio looked across the river again, pointing his chin toward Brownsville. "How're things over there, Hugh?"

"Not good. A lot of people were burned out, or lost

most of what they owned tryin' to get across the river. And it wasn't necessary. That's what makes it hurt so much, it wasn't necessary." His mood shifted from joy to momentary anger. "General Bee was in too much of a hurry about gettin' out of Brownsville. He listened to rumors, not to facts. Way it turned out, it was the third day after he left before the first Yankee troops got to town. Seemed there was a storm at the Boca Chica, and the soldiers had a hard time gettin' off of the boats. Bee could have brought all the refugees over here and ferried every single bale of cotton to boot. He could have hauled out every last bit of Confederate army supplies and not had to burn a single thing.

"But he got hold of bad information, and he panicked over it. Things would've been different if we'd had Rip Ford here."

Plunkett lighted a cigar, his face sober. "A lot of the Brownsville people have gone back home now to see what they've got left. They've decided the Yankees aren't goin' to shoot them. Them as go home are made to take an oath of allegiance to the Union. It don't mean much, though. I've taken an oath a dozen times to quit drinkin', and I ain't done it yet." He frowned. "One more thing. How do you stand with Juan Cortina?"

"I don't stand one way or the other. I only know him to see him."

"He's the top *tamali* around here now. While all the excitement was goin' on across the river, Cortina turned things upside down on this side. He shot General Cobos and has taken charge of Matamoros."

Frio's eyes narrowed. "He's no friend of the Confederacy. He might stop the border trade where the Yankees couldn't."

"I doubt that. It would mean too much loss to Matamoros. Cortina likes money even more than he hates Texans. He's on kissin' terms with the Yankees, but I expect he'll let the border trade go right ahead as long as there's profit in it. Just the same, he'll bear watchin'."

The ferry pulled up. Frio's gaze was drawn to the two passengers. One was a Union officer, a major. The other was Tom McCasland. They walked slowly up to the cottonyard. The officer's face twisted with displeasure as he regarded the wagons. Tom McCasland's face showed only sadness.

Tom held out his hand. "Frio."

Quietly Frio said, "Tom," and shook hands.

Tom said, "Major Quayle, meet Frio Wheeler."

The major gave no sign that he intended to shake hands, and Frio didn't press the issue by putting out his own. Quayle said, "Is he the one who brought in the wagons?"

Tom nodded. To Frio he said, "Patrol sent a man ahead, said a wagon train had gotten across at Don Andres's ferry. I figured right then it would be you, Frio. You're the only man I know with guts enough to try a stunt like that, and luck enough to get away with it."

Hugh Plunkett grinned at the open anger in the major's face. "Looks like you soldier boys got seasick for nothin', don't it, major?"

Major Quayle said crisply, "One wagon train doesn't mean anything. We were still a little disorganized. But this will be the last one, you can be assured of that. We'll patrol the river so that not even a hawk can get across it without our permission."

Frio squatted and leaned against a wagon wheel. With his finger he traced a rough map of lower Texas in the dust. "Major, you may know your maps, but you don't know the Rio Grande. You've got no idea what a long river she is till you wear blisters across your rump ridin' it. How much of it do you really think you can control? Up to Reynosa, maybe. Rio Grande City if you're real lucky. It's brush country, mister, plenty wild if you don't know its ways.

"No matter how far west you go, we'll go a little farther. You stop us here, we'll go to Rio Grande City. Stop us there and we'll go to Laredo to cross. We'll go as far as Eagle Pass if we have to. The point is, you won't stop our wagons. Do the damndest you know how, but we'll still keep them comin'."

The major's face colored, and his eyes snapped. "You secesh! You don't know when you're whipped!" He turned and stalked away. He went fifty feet, stopped, and turned back. "Are you coming, McCasland? We're going to talk to Cortina."

Tom nodded. "I'll be there in a minute." He looked at Frio again. "How's Amelia?"

"Tired out, last time I saw her, and still grievin' some. But she's in a safe place, and she'll be all right."

Tom said, "You're really goin' to keep the wagons comin', are you?"

"Just as sure as you're standin' there."

"Then there wasn't any use for the Union troops to come in, was there? Dad and all those others, they died for nothin'."

Somberly Frio replied, "It looks that way."

Tom's face clouded. "I warn you, Frio, we don't intend to leave it like that. One way or another, we intend to stop you!"

For a moment they stared into each other's eyes, neither man yielding. Frio said, "We won't be stopped. Don't try, Tom. I don't want to have to bury you!"

9

IN THE FOLLOWING WEEKS it gradually dawned upon Union General Dana in partially repaired Fort Brown that the federal occupation of Brownsville suffered serious shortcomings, that the "sealed-up" border had some bad holes in it. Slowly at first, then more and more frequently, Confederate wagon trains were appearing on the south bank of the river, hauling their heavy loads of cotton into the market at Matamoros, the teamsters gleefully thumbing their noses at the bluecoat troops north of the Rio.

That damnable Frio Wheeler had been only the first of them. Others, caught midway down from San Antonio by the sudden Union offensive, had simply been diverted upriver to points such as Rio Grande City. There they came under the protection of a bold troop of Texas-Mexican militia commanded by one Colonel Santos Benavides, whose watchful eyes stayed on the trains until they crossed over the river to safe ground. With Wheeler's lead to guide them, the *algodones* then followed the Mexican trail on down to Matamoros. True enough, the detour added many long miles to the haul from San Antonio. But the presence of the Yankees proved of little more than nuisance value. Within weeks the movement of cotton into Matamoros and the northward flow of imported war supplies was almost as large as it had ever been.

Once Dana sent a steamer upriver in hopes of cutting off some of the wagon crossings. But the drought still held, and the river was so shallow that sand bars stopped the vessel before it got as far as Roma.

He sent mounted troops to capture Rio Grande City, but they were unable even to reach there. Always they encountered the wily Benavides, his guerillalike troop of ranch-trained vaqueros darting in and out of the brush, striking with the swiftness of a rattlesnake and retreating into the chaparral so quickly that the federals hardly knew what had hit them. Pursuit was useless, for the Union cavalrymen knew little about the border country. If they strayed far from the river they might starve, for drought had left most of the waterholes dry. Benavides and his men knew the trails, knew the location of every single waterhole that still remained on the Wild Horse Desert.

Of course there were appeals to General Juan Cortina, who held control of Matamoros. Cortina had the power to cut off the cotton trade with a word, a single action. He professed his friendship for the Union, entertained Union officers in his quarters, and in turn was treated most cordially by Dana and his staff. The Mexican general even gave the Union officers full use of three Kennedy & Co. steamboats that had been registered under Mexican names and employed by the Confederacy. But he did not cut off the cotton trade. Though he hated Texans, he knew that so long as Matamoros prospered, he prospered. When it suffered, he would suffer. Without the border trade, Matamoros would sicken unto death.

This, then, was the situation in which Dana found himself. He held what was supposed to have been the key city, yet the enemy was outflanking him at points beyond his reach. He had several thousand troops at his command, while the Confederacy had at best only a few home guard units scattered along the entire stretch of the Mexican border. He could not send troops across into Mexico. The same restrictions that once had stopped the Confederacy now conspired to stop Dana. Nor could he touch the neutral vessels that flaunted the Union blockade by clustering around the mouth of the Rio Grande in full sight of federal gunboats. Even as it was, the Lincoln government had its hands full, trying to keep England and France from swinging the full weight of their support behind the Confederacy. An angry incident at the Boca Chica might be all that was needed to touch off an international crisis, to turn Europe against the United States.

To make it worse, spy reports indicated that the Texas Colonel Rip Ford was mustering troops in the San Antonio area, planning to come down and wrest the border away from the Union again. To be sure, Ford wouldn't be able to amass men in numbers equal to those of the federals—at least, Dana doubted it. But if they were all of the same caliber as those hard-riding Mexicans under Benavides, it wouldn't take as many.

The Union general, visiting the Matamoros side of the river, watched Frio Wheeler come into town with his second wagon train of cotton since the federal occupation. The man had thirty wagons with him this time. He was a wheelhorse, this blocky-built, dusty-faced, bewhiskered Texan. He had led the way, and others were following. Frio Wheeler was regarded by the Texans as a leader in the border trade, a man to follow, a man to imitate.

Well, the general thought grimly, to kill a snake you cut off its head!

And shortly afterward, Union Major Luther Quayle found himself seated at a dirty little table in a dark and odorous Matamoros cantina, staring across a flickering candle into the evil face of Florencio Chapa. . . .

Frio coughed as the south wind whipped up dust from the edge of the trail. He could imagine how much worse it must be in the drags, where Happy Jack Fleet was not so happy, bringing up the rear of Frio's train along the Mexican side of the river.

It seemed to Frio that this drought would never end. It conspired to make a difficult situation almost impossible—compounded the misery that already was bad enough, bringing these groaning wagons and these thirsting mules the long way around on a trail woefully short of feed. All winter he had watched Mexican teamsters on the oxcart trains, burning the thorns from prickly pear and feeding the pear to their oxen. But mules wouldn't eat prickly pear, with or without the thorns. So all winter Frio had had to devote space to maize and corn, space that would better have gone to cotton.

The river had receded to shoals in many places. Once he saw the steamer *Mustang* snagged on a sand bar. The Union officer in charge of troops aboard paced back and forth, swearing. The ship's crew was making signs of trying to free the little ship, but Frio knew their hearts weren't in it. Their loyalty remained with the Kennedy & Co. leadership and the Confederacy. They were doing only what they had to do for the Union, and taking their own sweet time about even that.

From the rear of the train, Happy Jack Fleet yelled at the troops, "Why don't you Yanks get off and push?"

What the soldiers yelled back at him was unintelligible, but its general meaning was plain enough.

The train's entry into Matamoros attracted much less attention than had the first one, only days after the Union had taken Brownsville. Frio understood this; Texas wagons were arriving in Matamoros almost every day now. They were becoming commonplace. Yet he was aware of one thing: People were looking upon him personally with an interest they had never shown before. He was the one who had first beaten the Yankees, the one who had shown the others the way. Suddenly he was no longer "Frio" as much as he was "Mr. Wheeler."

Coming up in the world, he thought, finding it somehow a little humorous. He hadn't sought this new importance, and he didn't take it very seriously.

He led the wagons into the Confederate cottonyard and shook hands with Hugh Plunkett. Plunkett grunted. "Brought me some more work, is all you done. Don't a man ever get any rest?"

"I haul it, you sell it. This war ever gets over with, maybe we can both rest."

Frio saw a young Union lieutenant in dusty blue leaning against a gatepost. Plunkett explained: "They got a man over here all the time now, not doin' a thing but watchin' what we do, countin' how much cotton we get, how much stuff we ship in and out. It don't do them any good to know—just makes them mad. Looks to me like they'd be happier just to stay ignorant."

Frio grinned. "You got anything around here to take the chill off a man? We used up our whole medicine supply on sick teamsters."

"Got some Scotch I swapped off of an English cotton buyer. It's in the shack yonder." He pointed toward a small frame building he was using as an office.

Frio walked up to the lieutenant. "Yank, we're fixin' to have us a drink. How about takin' one with us?"

The federal's face was blue from cold, and his eyes lighted at the prospect. Then he shook his head. "I don't drink with the enemy."

Frio said, "We're south of the river. There's no such thing here as enemies."

The officer glanced across the river as if he thought someone might be watching him from the other side. He hung back a moment, then nodded assent. "If you don't tell them, I won't. It can get almighty chilly here even if it is so far south."

In the shack Hugh Plunkett fetched out the bottle. There were no such refinements as glasses. They simply passed the bottle around. Frio watched warmth touch the young officer, putting a healthy color back into his pinched, blue face. He sat and pondered the foolishness, the contradictions of this war. If he and the officer were to meet on the other side of the river, they would try their best to kill each other. Here they sat together without enmity, taking the edge off their chill by drinking out of the same bottle.

Frio guessed this might be the deadliest war of its kind in history, with the friendliest enemies.

"Where you from, Lieutenant?"

"Illinois. We have a farm back there—my folks do, I mean."

Frio nodded. "My folks did some farmin' too, once, and raised stock. I've sort of got away from the plow, but I still raise cattle."

"We have milk stock," the lieutenant said. "Good-blooded cattle."

"Mine are just plain native cows," said Frio. "You couldn't get a bucket of milk out of a dozen of them."

The lieutenant was plainly homesick. And now the conversation had opened a way for him to begin talking about his home. He seemed oblivious to Frio—asked him questions and then went right on talking without giving time for an answer. He talked of the green fields of Illinois, his eyes going soft and blurry, and for a little while the war was forgotten. Frio just sat back and listened, seeing in his mind's eye the land the young officer described, knowing he would never get to go there and see it for himself. For a while, then, they were friends, and there was no war, no North or South.

At length the lieutenant squared his shoulders and handed the bottle back to Hugh Plunkett. "I guess I had better go. I have to count those bales."

Frio said, "I'll save you the trouble. There are thirty wagons, four hundred and eighty bales."

The officer stared quizzically. "That's military information. Why are you willing to tell me about it?"

"You'd get it anyway. Thought I'd save you the work."

The lieutenant smiled. "This is a crazy war."

When the Yankee was gone, Hugh offered Frio the bottle again. Frio declined. "We better be unloadin' those wagons."

Plunkett put away the bottle and turned, worry in

his eyes. "Frio, I don't know how you done it, but you've made yourself some good friends among these Mexicans. Do you remember an old fiddler, one they call Don Sisto?"

"I know him. I've done him a favor or two."

"He was over here. Said I better tell you Florencio Chapa's been seen around town. Rumor among the Mexicans is that he aims to kill you."

"He's tried before."

"Maybe this time he figures on doin' the job right. Was I you, Frio, I'd keep some good men around me, and I wouldn't sleep sound till I saw them shovelin' dirt in Chapa's face."

To the single men of the wagon train, Matamoros afforded a chance to relax from the grinding toil of the trails, to jam into crowded cantinas, get drunk on raw liquor, seek the warm excitement of some willing señorita. Those men who had homes here or in Brownsville could spend a couple or three nights with their wives and children. The Mexican teamsters passed with comparative freedom back and forth across the river, for to the Yankees one brown face looked like another. To Anglos like Frio and Happy Jack, however, the river was a barrier they dared not cross. They could only stand on the south bank and gaze across at the lamplight of Brownsville, sadly remembering the time when they had not been in exile.

Frio intended to spend a couple or three days in Matamoros before starting the long return trip upriver. The mules needed rest. They needed green feed, too, but they couldn't get it. Frio wished he could loose-herd them on grass a few days and let them fill their bellies. There was no chance. The long drought had left little grass. And the Mexicans with their own herds of cattle, their countless burros and scrubby horses, had kept the land so overstocked that it would be a long time before there was feed enough again.

So, in lieu of pasture grazing, he turned his mules loose in a big brush-fence corral, for which he had paid the owner a small rental. He fed them all they wanted of hay, which he bought from a few Mexicans who irrigated small fields out of the river. He circled the empty wagons outside the corral and set up his camp.

He remembered what Hugh Plunkett had told him about Chapa, but he had never felt unsafe in Matamoros. He thought it unfair to make a bunch of the young men forgo the city's pleasure and stay for his protection. He let all of them go except a small guard of three, who would remain around camp, mostly to prevent pilfering. These three would be chosen each night by the men themselves, cutting cards. The married men with families here were exempt. Besides the three young men, a couple of the older ones elected to remain in camp. Both had families in San Antonio and considered themselves too far along in years to work up a fever over the flashing eyes and pinched-in waists of the dark-haired señoritas. They were content to buy a bottle and stay with the wagons.

Like these men, Frio felt little urge to try the night life. The pressures of being wagon boss had worn him out. He only wanted to rest. Besides, there was Amelia.

He got a chuckle, watching Happy Jack. Happy was shaved, bathed, his hair plastered down with grease and smelling to heaven of something they had sprinkled on his new clothes down at the barber shop.

He stood in the firelight, admiring the cut of his coat and trousers.

"You sure you don't want to come along, Frio? Margarita has got a sister, and she's . . . Well, you've got to see it to appreciate it. You never saw anything like her."

Frio smiled. "I probably have. I've been around longer than you."

"You're lettin' yourself go to seed, is what you're doin'. Man, you just got one life. You better live it."

"Maybe you best take care of Margarita *and* her sister."

The young man laughed. "I haven't got *that* much life about me."

Happy walked out of the firelight and disappeared in the direction of the city. Slowly the rest of the men scattered too. Soon only Frio and the two *viejos* were left, and the three unlucky young ones who were to guard the wagons. Frio let the fire burn down almost to coals, so that it still put out heat but shed little light. He was wary enough not to make an easy target of himself.

He sat and stared into the coals, watching their kaleidoscopic change of colors as the heat built and waned. Listening to the night sounds of the Mexican city, he let his mind trail back to other times—to Brownsville and Matamoros as they had been before the war, to Amelia and Tom and Meade McCasland, to the ranch he and Tom had so hopefully started. He considered his own sacrifices and knew they were small compared to those made by so many others. Many men of his acquaintance had already given their lives for the South. He, at least, was still alive, still had his ranch and his cattle. And he had Amelia. When this war was over he would have something to go home to.

From what he knew of the campaign in Virginia, thousands of men would have no home left.

He sat there remembering, and lost track of time. He was aware of the two older men turning up their bottle and dropping it on the ground empty. They weaved unsteadily toward their blankets. A guard came up and spoke to Frio and poured himself a cup of coffee from the pot at the edge of the coals.

They heard someone approaching. The guard straightened, gun in hand. He said in Spanish, "Some of the boys coming back, probably. The foolish ones do not know how to take their time and make a night last." He called out, *"Quién viva?"* Who goes there?

A Mexican voice responded from beyond the ragged edge of firelight. "Señor Wheeler? I seek the Señor Wheeler."

Frio arose and drew his six-shooter, keeping well back in darkness. "Come ahead, with your hands away from your sides. Stop by the fire."

In the dim glow of the embers he could see that this was a stranger with wide sombrero, open leather huaraches and the loose cotton clothing of the *peón*. "I have come with a message for the Señor Wheeler," the man said, taking his hat in his hands. He shivered from cold.

"Are you by yourself?" Frio asked suspiciously. .

"Sí, señor."

The guard went to look. In a moment he was back. "He is alone, *patrón*."

Frio said, "What is it you want of me?"

"You have a young friend, a gringo with hair the color of sand?"

Frio stiffened. Happy Jack! "What about him?"

"He is in trouble, señor. There has been a fight, a bad fight, and he is hurt. He needs your help."

Alarm raced in Frio. But there was also doubt. "Who sent you?"

"A friend of the boy. A woman."

That added up, Frio thought. Still, there was an off chance this could be a lie, a ruse. "Where is Happy now?"

"He is in the woman's house. He asked for you. It is possible he dies, señor."

Frio could not hesitate long, even though a lingering doubt persisted. To the guard he said, "Felix, I had better go with him."

He could tell that the guard, too, had his doubts. "I will go with you, *patrón*. The other two can guard the wagons. They have the *viejos* for help."

"Thanks, Felix," Frio said gratefully. "Happy might need both of us."

They paused only long enough to let the other two guards know where they were going. They trailed out into the darkness afoot, following the man who had brought the message. Frio kept the six-shooter in his hand, ready. Felix did likewise. It occurred to Frio belatedly that Felix was one of the poorest marksmen in the crew. He hoped the teamster never had to use that gun.

The Mexican led them through narrow alleys, down dark streets. Dogs picked them up and trotted alongside, barking and making false runs at them. Candlelight flickered inside tiny brush *jacales*, leaking though cracks in the walls and doors.

"How much farther is it?" Frio asked. "If I had known it was this far, I'd have brought a horse."

"Not far now, señor," the man said and kept walking,

Frio didn't like the neighborhood. Dark doorways frowned upon the narrow dirt streets, doorways big enough to hide waiting men in their deep shadows. He kept to the center of the street.

He wondered at even the reckless Happy Jack coming into a section like this.

At last the Mexican pointed. "This is the place." He reached for a latch and swung the wooden door inward. "*Pasen*, señores."

Frio gripped the six-shooter a little tighter, peered a brief moment into the Mexican's face, then stepped through the open door toward the guttering light of a small candle.

Too late he sensed that the thing was all wrong. Too late he saw the dark shapes step away from the wall. He spun, bringing the pistol around. Someone shoved him from behind, and he went stumbling across the dirt floor. Heavy bodies landed on top of him almost the moment his shoulder struck earth. A boot stomped his wrist. Rough hands tore the pistol from his fingers, taking some of the hide with it.

He heard a dull thud as a sombreroed man clubbed Felix from behind with the butt of a rifle. Felix went to his knees. The rifle barrel swung savagely and struck Felix across the back of the head. The teamster went down like an empty sack. His blood made a dark stain on the dirt floor.

A harsh voice said in Spanish, "You hit him too hard, Florencio. He is dead."

Florencio Chapa shrugged and snarled, "It is a just punishment for any Mexican who carries a gun for a gringo. Be sure he is dead before you drag him away. If there is any doubt, shoot him behind the ear."

"There is no doubt, *mi jefe*."

"Then drag him out of here. Leave him somewhere for the dogs."

In anger Frio tried to arise, tried to reach Chapa.

Strong hands restrained him. Chapa waited until Frio's face was turned up to his own, the eyes flashing hatred. Then he kicked. Frio twisted away, but the heavy boot caught him on the side of the head.

"So you came for your friend," Chapa gloated. "Like a rabbit to the wolf's den, you came."

Held tightly, Frio could do nothing but watch as a couple of the men dragged Felix's body out into the darkness. The door closed behind them. Eyes glazing from the pain of the blow he had received, Frio blinked hard. Helpless anger surged through him. He knew he had to curb that anger, had to keep his head. Rage was a luxury he could not afford now.

He looked at the men standing around the wall. There were four of them besides Chapa, and besides the two men who held him down. One was the gringo renegade, Bige Campsey.

Campsey smiled crookedly. "I been listenin' to you rebs talk for two years. Thought I'd enjoy listenin' to one of you scream awhile."

Frio had often wondered why Chapa, hating gringos so passionately, allowed Campsey to ride with him almost as a partner. Perhaps it was that he sensed in Campsey a kindred spirit, a senseless sadism that transcended any national barriers.

Chapa said, "Stand him up!" The two men pulled Frio to his feet. Chapa smiled. It was a cold, cruel smile, the *bandido*'s eyes like those of a snake. "You owe me two thousand dollars, Frio Wheeler. I am going to collect in blood!" He laughed harshly. "You gringos are stupid, the *yanqui* army as stupid as the rest of you. They could do nothing about you, so tonight they gave me money to get rid of you. Fools! I was about to do it for nothing."

Frio said in disbelief, "They paid you?"

Chapa nodded. "A very funny joke, *sí*?"

His fist darted. Frio tried to turn away but could not. Fire flashed before his eyes as the blow struck him full in the face. He tasted blood.

Chapa ordered crisply, "Off with his coat and shirt. Tie his hands." They tore the clothing from him, down to the waist. He struggled against them, but they stamped the breath out of him and then tied his hands with rawhide so tightly that he knew the circulation would be badly impaired. They stood him with his stomach to the wall, stretching his hands overhead and tying them by the rawhide thong to the rafter above him.

Chapa had a whip. He flipped away the coils and snapped the end of it. "You are a mule driver, amigo. You know how to use a whip on mules. Now see how it feels to you!"

Frio shrank against the wall as the lash cut into his back. He wanted to cry out but managed to control himself.

"Scream if you want to," said Chapa. "No one will hear you—no one who cares." He struck again. The lash was like fire. Frio's knees sagged.

Chapa said, "You will think you are going to die. You will wish you *could* die. But I do not intend to let you go too soon. You are going to die slowly, gringo. You are going to die a two-thousand-dollar death."

Chapa quit talking and used his strength in swinging the whip. Each time, Frio thought he would scream, thought he could not stand one more. Cold sweat stood on his face. Teeth clamped, fists knotted, he cringed against the wall each time he heard the cruel hiss of the lash starting to move.

He was no more than half conscious when they cut

him down. He fell heavily to the dirt floor. They threw cold water into his face.

"Bring him outside," said Chapa. "We will see how well he drags."

On his hands and knees, Frio watched, while Chapa mounted a splendid horse in the dim starlight—a stolen horse, without doubt. Chapa took down a rawhide rope from the big horn of his Mexican saddle and pitched the loop end out to Bige Campsey. Campsey put it around Frio's arms and jerked up the slack. Dallying the reata around the horn, Chapa touched wicked spurs to his horse. Frio was jerked forward onto his stomach. He felt himself dragging in the street, blunt rocks bruising him, tearing his skin.

The dragging stopped for a moment. Chapa came back in a lope, the big horse barely missing Frio. The *bandido* hit the end of the rope and jerked Frio around backward, dragging him again. Sixty or seventy feet and he stopped once more.

Head pounding, his body ablaze with pain, Frio knew he couldn't last much longer. Another drag or two and he would be unconscious, or nearly so. If he was to fight back, he had to do it now. He pushed to his hands and knees as Chapa turned the horse around for another run. Frio's hands were still bound, but his fingers closed over the rawhide rope and went tight.

Chapa spurred and came running. Frio waited, his heart pounding desperately. When Chapa was almost upon him, Frio arose on wobbly legs and flipped the slack in the rope. He saw it go around the horse's forefeet. He turned his body into the rope, hands behind him, binding the rope across his hip. He saw Chapa desperately claw a pistol from its holster and at the same time try to rein the running horse to a stop.

The Mexican was too late. The horse was running

full tilt when its feet tangled in the reata. The rope came suddenly tight, and the jar of it sent Frio to his knees again. But he had done what he had hoped. The horse went down threshing, on top of Chapa. The barrel of the pistol drove deep into the dirt. Frio pushed to his feet and ran unsteadily. He was aware of Chapa's men shouting and surging toward him. But he was much closer to Chapa then they were.

On his side, his legs pinned under the still struggling horse, Chapa swung the pistol around. He held it in both hands, near his face. He aimed it point-blank, and Frio felt the heart drop out of him. Chapa squeezed the trigger.

The gunbarrel was jammed full of dirt, and the pistol exploded with a blinding flash. Chapa screamed in agony, clasping both bleeding hands across his face. Blood flowed out between the broken fingers.

The horse was struggling to its feet. With the little strength still in him, Frio swung into the saddle. The *bandidos* came running, Bige Campsey in the lead. Frio drummed his heels against the horse's ribs and hoped the animal didn't step on the long reata that trailed from Frio's wrists. Frightened, the horse broke into a run. He faltered a little, for the fall had hurt him. Frio kicked him again to keep him running. The bandits ran along behind, afoot. Frio bent low in the saddle, knowing they would shoot at him but hoping the darkness would protect him until he could get around the rock buildings down the street.

He heard the slugs whine by his head. For a moment he thought he was going to get away clean.

Then the bullet struck him in the back, deep in the shoulder. He reeled in the saddle, almost fell to the ground. His fingers grabbed desperately for the big horn of Chapa's saddle. They closed around it, and he managed to catch himself.

Moments later he realized dully that he was in the clear. The bullet was like a heavy, glowing coal in his shoulder. He felt his blood running down his bare back. It took all the determination he could muster to hold himself in the saddle. But somewhere yonder, somewhere ahead of him in the night, lay his wagon camp. He clenched his teeth in agony and swore to himself that he would stay alive until he found his wagons.

10

Tom McCasland rapped his knuckles gently against the wooden door. A voice answered, "Come in." Tom pushed the door open and saw Major Luther Quayle seated behind a table that served as a desk. Quayle stood up in pleased surprise.

"You didn't waste any time getting here."

"Came as soon as I got the word," Tom replied. He strode across and shook hands. The major reached behind some rolled maps on a shelf and brought out a bottle. He gripped a pair of small glasses between his thumb and two fingers. He poured the glasses full and handed one to Tom.

"This," he said, "is the only thing that makes life endurable in this godforsaken assignment."

Tom said, "You didn't call me over here to drink."

"No, but a drink might help. You'll need another one or two before I'm through."

"You must have a tough job for me this time."

Quayle only frowned, not making an answer. He sat on the corner of the table, his eyebrows knitted, and he studied Tom McCasland with a keen eye. Tom flinched, uncomfortable under the penetrating gaze.

"McCasland, you have a good reputation with us. When we came, you told us you would do anything for the Union. Up to now you've done everything we asked of you and never held back for a moment." He scowled down at his near-empty glass. "Now I'm afraid we're about to put you to the supreme test. Before I tell you what it is, I'll say this: We didn't want to ask you. We've tried alternatives, to no avail."

Tom said, "I'm a soldier, of sorts. I won't turn away from danger."

Quayle poured himself another drink. Tom waved the major away when he reached for Tom's glass. Quayle took a long swallow, obviously dreading what he was to say. "It's not so much the danger that concerns us."

He set the glass down and turned away from Tom. "McCasland, you're a longtime friend of this Frio Wheeler, aren't you?"

"From a long way back. We used to be partners."

"You know he's been a thorn in our side. You know he's a kingpin in the border trade."

"I know all that."

"Did you know he was badly wounded in Matamoros a couple of nights ago?"

Tom sat up straight. "No! How bad?"

"Bad. But for us, not bad enough. He's still alive."

Tom breathed out a sigh of relief. Quayle turned to frown at him. "I can understand your feelings, McCasland. He's your friend. But at the same time, he's our enemy. It would have been better for us if he had died."

"How did it happen?"

"That bandit Chapa." Quayle pushed away from the table. "You won't like this, McCasland, but I think you'll understand why we tried it. We paid Chapa to kill him." When Tom's eyes widened in quick anger, Quayle explained, "Wheeler stays out of our reach. So long as he's across the river, not a hand can be raised against him—by us. But by a Mexican, that's another matter. Through our intelligence work we found out that there was bad blood between Wheeler and this Chapa. We thought that with a little extra incentive, Chapa would take care of the matter for us, and our hands would have been clean." He paused. "They would have *looked* clean, anyway. Hell, everybody knows war is a dirty business.

"What we didn't count on was Chapa's method. We assumed he would do the job the way we would, the quickest way possible to get it over with. But no, he wanted to do it by torture. He wanted Wheeler to die a slow death."

Quayle glanced at Tom again and looked quickly away from the steady, cold gaze he encountered. "If we'd known he was going to do it like that, we wouldn't have gone to him at all. We don't sanction torture, McCasland. Be that as it may, Chapa became so eager in his work that he got careless. Somehow Wheeler tripped Chapa's horse and made it fall on him. Wheeler dragged himself onto the horse and got away.

"Not completely away, though. That"—his nose wrinkled with disgust—"that *patriot* Campsey was there, and he wounded Wheeler as your friend rode off. Best we can tell from our intelligence reports, it was a rather bad wound, somewhere in the shoulder. Wheeler lost a lot of blood, but he got back to his camp. His men brought a Mexican doctor and saved him from bleeding to death. They took him across the river in a boat, in the night, and put him on a wagon right under our noses. They hauled him to his ranch." He scowled. "If all the secesh were that hard to kill, we never could win this war."

Tom said, "I heard his wagons moved out with a load of supplies this mornin', bound upriver. I thought he was with them. . . ."

Quayle shook his head. "He has a young fellow working for him—Fleet, I think the name is. *He* took the wagons. You can bet that if we don't find a way to stop Wheeler he'll be back with that train as soon as he has the strength to ride."

The officer poured Tom's glass full. "Better drink that, McCasland, before I tell you the rest."

Tom sipped suspiciously.

Quayle said, "This occupation of Brownsville has been a severe disappointment to us, as you surely know. We thought all we had to do was take the town and we would stop the Confederate border trade. It didn't work that way. All we've done is inconvenience them. The trade goes on while we stand here helplessly and watch.

"The key to it is the wagon trains. They stay pretty well out of our reach. Our troops don't know this country, and they can't do much by themselves. That's why we've hired all the border renegades we can find to help us, to guide our patrols to the striking points and back again. We do all we can to disrupt those trails. But the wagons keep coming. The reason is the influence of a few key men. Captain Richard King is one. Your friend Wheeler is another. King isn't my problem; someone else has that assignment. But Wheeler *is* my problem. I won't have a moment's peace until that man is dead."

Tom took the rest of the drink and stared again at the floor. "I don't know why you called on me. You know I can't help you."

"Wrong, McCasland, you *can*. The question is, will you?" The major walked around the table and stood directly in front of Tom. "We are reasonably certain that Wheeler is at his ranch right now, wounded. He's vulnerable. We doubt strongly that he has a guard that would give us any real trouble. Our only problem is to get there. We didn't want to ask your help on this, McCasland. We've tried for most of two days to find someone who would guide us to Wheeler's ranch. But the Mexicans who know the way are loyal to him or afraid of the others who are. We can't find one who will take us. You're our only hope."

Tom stood up, angry. He placed the glass on the table and strode stiffly across the room to peer out the window. "Major, what kind of a Judas do you take me for? Send me out on any decent kind of a job— I've never turned you down yet. But to do a thing like this. . . ." He shook his head violently. "Court-martial me if you want to, I won't do it."

Quayle said sympathetically, "I expected you to be angry. But I also thought that when you considered it, you'd see why we had to ask you. Sure, I know he's your friend. That's what makes this war so monstrous, McCasland—we're fighting men who were our friends, even our blood kin." A sadness came into his eyes. "I had a cousin when I grew up. He was more than kin, he was the best friend I had. But when the war started we went separate ways. I chose the blue and he chose the gray. I saw him after Shiloh, dead. For all I know, my own bullet could have killed him.

"This is my point: Every day that the war goes on means more men dead on the battlefields. Every day by which we can shorten this war means that many men saved. Now, I'm not claiming that this border trade is the major factor keeping the Confederacy alive; it isn't. But it is *one* of the factors. If we can stop it, the Confederacy dies sooner—by days, maybe weeks, perhaps even months. No one can say how many lives would be saved. Thousands, maybe. Your friend is one of the keys. If we kill him, we can save men who otherwise would have died."

Quayle placed his hand on Tom's shoulder. "Think, McCasland. Think with your head, not with your heart. Is your friendship with this one man worth the lives of thousands? Would you stand by and see them die because you lacked the strength to kill one man?"

Tom swallowed. He stared out the window a long time. "God, Major, you make it hard."

"No one ever claimed war was easy."

"Whichever way I go, I'll regret it to the day I die."

"Our side didn't start this war."

Tom shook his head. "Who did? I guess when it's over we'll find that none of us was completely guilty, and none of us innocent."

"It's your decision to make, McCasland."

Tom rubbed his hand across his face. Misery dulled his voice. "I'd rather be dead than make it."

Luisa Valdez stood in the doorway that led to the tiny candlelit bedroom and stared with narrowed, worried eyes at Tom McCasland. Tom sat slumped in a chair, gripping a bottle of whisky at the neck. His eyes had long since gone glazed. Luisa walked over slowly and took the bottle.

"Tom, don't you think you've had enough?"

Shaking his head, he pulled the bottle out of her grasp. She took a step backward, raising her hand and touching a forefinger to the corner of her eye, wiping away a stray tear.

"Tom, I've never seen you like this. You've never been a hard drinker. What's wrong?"

Tom made no sign he had heard her. His eyes stared blankly off into the distance.

Luisa moved in again and placed her hand against his cheek. "Is it something I have done, something I have said? I didn't know I had done anything to displease you. I didn't mean to."

The sadness in her voice seemed to move him. He looked up at her and shook his head. "No, Luisa, it isn't you. You could never do anything to displease me."

She leaned down and kissed him on the forehead. "Then it can't be anything so bad that you want to drink yourself to sleep. Come on, Tom, let's go to bed. You'll feel better tomorrow."

He shook his head. "Once I do what I have to, I doubt if I'll ever sleep again, unless I drink myself to it."

Alarm showed in her eyes. "What have they asked you to do this time, Tom? Is it something dangerous again?"

"Dangerous? No, not especially. Not for me, anyway."

"Then don't let it trouble you so." She kissed him again. "Forget it for now. We'll go to bed."

He studied her with a brooding gaze. "You may not

feel that way about me after tomorrow. You may have nothing but contempt for me."

Luisa stiffened. "Tom, what sort of job have they given you?"

Tom's head tilted over. He stared at the floor a minute, then took another long drink. "They're sending me to kill Frio Wheeler."

Luisa gasped. "Tom, you can't!"

"I never would have thought I could. But they've shown me that it has to be done. I'm the one who must do it."

Hands over her face, Luisa walked slowly to the bedroom door and turned. "But why?"

"Because his death could shorten the war. Maybe not much, but even a few days would save a great many men. One man's life against all those others. When you look at it that way, you see why it has to be done."

"Not just one man's life, Tom. He's your friend. When you destroy him, you'll also destroy yourself."

"All right, *two* men. What are we worth, two of us against all those who might be saved?"

"What of your sister, Tom? She's in love with him. Maybe you don't realize it, but I saw it that night at the *fandango*. You'll break her heart."

"She's young."

"She'll hate you."

Angrily he shouted, "For God's sake, Luisa, don't you think I know that? Don't you think I've run it through my brain a thousand times already? Why do you think I've been nursing this bottle all night? Maybe if I drink enough I can blot all these things out of my mind. Maybe if I'm drunk enough I can do what I have to without my conscience dragging me back.

Maybe if I stay drunk afterward I won't have to listen to my conscience at all."

Luisa dropped down upon a chair and began to sob. Presently the empty bottle fell clattering to the floor. Looking up, she found that Tom had slumped over, asleep. Slowly she pushed to her feet, stooping to pick up the fallen bottle. She stared a while at the sleeping man and blinked back tears. Finally, making up her mind, she wrapped a heavy woolen shawl around her shoulders and went out into the chilly night.

She started up the dark street, walking hurriedly. A pair of Union soldiers stepped in front of her before she reached the main plaza. She brushed past them, ignoring their remarks, thinking that it was hard to tell much difference between Confederate soldier and Yankee when they came across the river to Matamoros. Or Mexican soldiers, either, for that matter. Their wants were simple and predictable.

She was uncertain which house was the one she sought. She chose one and nervously rapped on the wooden door. She saw a light flicker as someone brought flame to a candle from banked coals in the fireplace. The door opened partway and a man's head showed against the dim light. His eyes widened at the sight of the slender woman standing there.

"Hello," he said. "You sure you got the right house?"

"I am looking for the Señor Plunkett."

He stammered. "W . . . well, I'm him, but I sure didn't send for you."

"I must talk with you. It is most urgent, about Señor Wheeler."

Plunkett said, "Give me a minute to get some pants on, then come on in.

He was buttoning his shirt when she entered the room. He modestly turned away until he had the last button done, all the way to the collar. "Now, what's this about Frio?"

"You must send someone to warn him. They are going to his place to kill him."

Plunkett's mouth dropped open. "Who?"

"The *yanqui* soldiers. Tom McCasland is going to take them."

"McCasland?' Incredulous, Plunkett said, "But he's Frio's friend." He stared at her, not knowing whether to believe her or not. Recognition slowly came to him. "I know you. You're Señora Valdez. I've seen you with McCasland." His eyes narrowed. "Tom McCasland's your man. Why would you come and tell me this?"

The tears started again, and she turned half away. "To save Tom. They tell him he must do it for his country. But if he helps them to kill his friend, Tom will die too, inside. I would save him that."

"He ever finds out you came and told me, you're liable to lose him."

"At least I will know he is not eating his own heart away, remembering that he killed his best friend. Better to lose him and know he is alive than to have him and know that the spirit in him is dead."

Plunkett nodded slowly, his eyes grave. "You're a brave woman, Señora Valdez. You made the right choice. I know a man who can make the ride. He'll leave before daylight."

She turned toward the door, her shoulders slumped. "Thank you, Señor Plunkett."

He let her get halfway through the door before he said, "I promise you one thing: Nobody will ever find out from me how I knew about this."

She said, "Thank you, señor. But Tom will know anyway. He will guess."

She disappeared into the night.

11

THE ROUGH ROCK WALLS were without ornamentation of any kind—not a picture, not a crucifix. In his first hours here, Frio had lain with a blazing fever and stared with glazed eyes at the dark door of death, which had loomed wide and open in the gloom just beyond the foot of the bed. Later, fever subsiding but the bedclothes still sticking to his body, he had studied those bare walls until he knew every crack, every little squeeze of mortar. In their rough shape and from the shadows that lay across them he could make out vague pictures of faces and mountains and horses and cattle.

Most of the fever was gone now, though a lingering weakness continued to hold him down. He was tired of lying here this way when there was so much that needed to be done. Experimentally he swung his legs off the cot and let his bare feet touch the earthen floor.

His head swirled. He had to hold it in his hands. The wound began to throb afresh.

Cooking in the other room, Amelia McCasland heard him move. She dropped a stirring spoon into an iron pot and came to see about him. Frio pulled the blanket up to cover himself.

"Frio," she scolded, "you lie back and be still. You'll break that wound open again."

His head was swimming so much that it was hard to keep his eyes on her. "Just wanted to see how I'd feel sittin' up. I can't stay in bed forever."

"You'll stay there awhile longer if you want to live. Now lie down!"

Grudgingly he pulled his feet up and stretched out again. It was true he felt much better this way. He doubted he could get to the front door afoot. He had lost a lot of blood.

"I've got to be up and out with my wagons."

"Happy Jack can take care of the wagons for one trip, at least."

Frio's face twisted. A glowing anger had remained banked inside him since the night Florencio Chapa had so coldly killed Felix and had put the whip to Frio. "Just takin' care of them isn't enough. I want those wagons to roll far and fast. I want to show the Yankees how much war goods I can haul. I want to show them I'm a long way from bein' dead—that they wasted the blood money they paid Chapa."

Amelia said, "You're hating too hard, Frio. Hate is a cruel master." She sat on the edge of the cot, put her warm hand gently to his face, and tried to force a smile. "Try to put the hatred away. Be glad you can lie back and rest. Be glad you can spend some time here with me."

He reached up and took her hand. "You know

people are goin' to talk, you stayin' in the same house with me."

"The condition you're in, what could happen?" She wrinkled her nose. "It'll take more than talk to hurt me anymore. Anyway, I'll let you make an honest woman of me anytime you want to."

He tightened his grip on her hand. "Someday, Amelia, when I can, I'll take you with me down to Matamoros. We'll be married there."

She leaned down and kissed him. "I'm only sorry it took a bullet in the back to make you say that."

Someone knocked at the front door. Blas Talamantes and his wife came into the house. María carried a tin bucket of milk. Blas strode directly into the bedroom, taking off his big sombrero. "Ah, Frio, you feel a little better, no?"

Frio nodded. "Some. How is everything goin'?"

Blas shrugged. "*Bueno*. The cattle are thin, but mostly they still live. Maybeso it rains in the spring."

Standing in the doorway, María held up the bucket. "*Madama*, I have bring milk for the *patrón*. It will help to make him well."

Frio grimaced. "Milk!"

María said, "You need it. You must drink it for strong."

Frio argued. "You need it worse than I do, María. You're drinkin' it for two." The tiny woman was showing her pregnancy more every day.

Blas placed his strong arm around his wife's thin shoulder. "I burn prickly pear for the milk cow. Pear makes for plenty milk. We get enough for María and for you, too, don't you worry."

María's fingers went up to touch Blas's hand, and she leaned her head down so that her cheek rested against the man's arm. She said, "So long as I have Blas, I have no need for anything else."

Blas smiled down at her. In the moment of silence, Frio heard a running horse. Blas heard it too, for he turned his head to listen. The boy Chico burst through the door. Bundled in a coat twice too large for him, he had been playing outdoors.

He said excitedly, "Somebody is come!"

Through the open door they heard a man outside shouting, "Blas! Blas Talamantes!" It was a Mexican voice.

Blas stepped to the door and hailed the man. "*Aquí*, Natividad. Slow down a little. You live much longer."

Natividad de la Cruz stepped hurriedly up onto the little porch. "There is no time to slow down. The *yanqui* soldiers, they are not far behind me. Where is the Frio?"

Blas's smile was wiped away in a second. "Frio is here, in bed. We cannot move him."

"The *yanquis* will do more than move him!"

Natividad, about the same age as Blas, was a one-time vaquero who worked for Hugh Plunkett in the cottonyard. Once Frio had brought medicine all the way from San Antonio for Natividad's sick wife. She had died anyway, but the man's gratitude had never changed. Natividad brushed past Blas and hurried to the bedroom.

"Mr. Frio, you get away from here quick! The *yanquis*, they come for to kill you!"

The color left Amelia's face. Frio demanded, "How do you know?"

"Señor Plunkett, he say for me to ride like the wind. My horse he is go lame, and the soldiers they pass me while I am finding another. I spur him hard and go around them, but they follow close. You got very little time."

Frio sat up shakily and put his feet on the floor again. Amelia protested, "Frio, you can't go, not in your condition. Let them arrest you. What can they do?"

Natividad said, "Pardon me, señorita, but Señor Plunkett he say they don't come to arrest him, they come for to kill him!"

Amelia cried, "You can't ride a horse, Frio. You'll tear that wound open and bleed to death!"

"I can't just lie here!"

Blas had listened gravely. Now, voice urgent, he said, "I fix. Miss Amelia, you and María and Natividad, you take Frio out into the thick brush. Go as far as you can. Wipe out your tracks behind you. I take Natividad's horse and lead the *yanquis* away."

He dropped his sombrero on the floor and took one of Frio's hats from a peg on the wall. He slipped off his Mexican coat and put on one of Frio's.

Frio shook his head. "Too risky. I won't let you do it."

Blas said sternly, "You can't stop me. Hurry up now, all of you. *Ándele!*"

Natividad helped Frio pull on a pair of pants and get boots on his feet. Frio tried to stand alone but swayed and nearly fell. Natividad caught and steadied him, pulling Frio's good arm around his shoulder to give him support. He flung a blanket over Frio's back to keep him warm when they went out into the chill of the open air.

Tearful, María clutched at her husband. "Blas, Blas, don't do it!"

"Don't worry, *querida*. It is pretty soon dark. They

will think I am Frio. I let them follow, but I don't let them get close."

María cried, "Blas, they will kill you!"

He threw his arms around her and crushed her to him. He kissed her, then pushed her away. "Go now. No *yanqui* soldier can kill me, not when I have a son on the way that I have not even seen."

Blas hurried out to see about Natividad's horse. Frio said, "Amelia, bring the rifle!" She got it. With Natividad to help her, she brought Frio out into the fading afternoon. The chill cut him at first like the sharp edge of a knife. María hurried along behind, carrying several warm blankets over one arm. She clutched Chico's hand and dragged the boy in a run. She paused a moment to look back at her husband, who stood beside the horse, awaiting first sight of the Union soldiers.

"Blas," she called brokenly, "go with God!"

He blew his wife a kiss and watched her until she and the others disappeared south into the brush. Blas turned then and kept his gaze on the Brownsville trail. A cold sweat broke across his face. It wasn't long, perhaps ten minutes, when he saw the first bluecoat push warily out of the brush. Shortly he could see forty or fifty troopers. Their officer gave a signal. The soldiers spurred into a run toward the house.

Blas waited only long enough to cross himself. Then he swung into the saddle and broke north, putting Natividad's tiring horse into a lope. Blas purposely hunched over in the saddle, the way a wounded man would. It stood to reason they knew Frio was wounded, else why would they have come?

Looking over his shoulder, he saw that they were following him as hard as they could run.

Blas gritted his teeth and tore into the brush.

* * *

Tom McCasland had ridden in torture all day. The whisky he had drunk last night still burned in his belly like a bank of coals, and his head throbbed as if someone were crushing his skull with a sledge. He had no recollection of going to bed. The last he remembered, he had still been sitting up in a chair. He hadn't awakened until the impatient Major Quayle had sent someone this morning to find out why he hadn't reported when he was supposed to. The major had ridden beside him in angry silence all day. Because of Tom, the patrol had been delayed more than an hour beyond its scheduled starting time. Twice they had to stop and allow Tom to be sick. Small wonder Quayle was disgusted with him.

Well, Tom thought, what had they expected, asking him to do a job like this? They couldn't expect a man to help kill his best friend and do it cold sober.

For a while last night the liquor had at least numbed the edge of his guilt. Now nothing was left but the dregs of the whisky, and the guilt was with him again, riding upon his shoulders with the weight of stone. It shrieked in his ear like some querulous old beggar-woman at the city plaza, berating a passerby for dropping no coin in her outstretched hand.

When the war was over, he would have to leave this part of the country; he knew that. He realized he would be regarded from now on as a Judas. He could never hope to make people understand. His friends would turn away, loathing him. And his sister. . . . He shook his head sadly at thought of her. When Frio died, Amelia would reject Tom with a hatred that probably would last the rest of her life.

Yet, he knew what his duty was, and he would do it. But at what a cost!

Perhaps when the war was over he would change his name. Maybe he would go west to California, for that was a new and growing land. Or even down into Mexico. He knew the Mexican people well, and by now he spoke their language almost as they did. He could start fresh.

Or could he? Did a man ever really start fresh? No matter where he went, no matter if he changed his surroundings, his clothes, even his language, he would take his memories with him. He would take with him the cancerous guilt that eroded his soul. Not even the love of a woman like Luisa Valdez would be enough to offset that.

Luisa! He remembered the shock in her face last night when he had told her what he was going to do. She could not have been more shaken if he had struck her with his fist. He had half expected her to turn her back on him and call him a betrayer. Yet, this morning she had seemed strangely calm. She hadn't tried to argue with him. That was one thing about most Mexican women: They believed it was the man's place to make the decisions. Right or wrong, they followed him.

"It's getting late," Major Quayle said. It was the first time he had spoken to Tom in a couple of hours. "How much farther?"

"We're almost there. We'll break out of this brush in a minute and into the clearing where the houses are."

The major turned to the sergeant. "Get the men closed up. Tell them to have their carbines ready. We'll go in running. We'll give them no time to set up a defense."

Tom said bitterly, "Who? A wounded man, a couple of women, maybe one or two Mexicans? Remember what I told you, Major: My sister is there. I don't want her hurt."

"We'll get this over with in a hurry. She won't be hurt."

Won't be hurt! The major's words struck Tom like some sardonic joke. Killing Frio was the worst hurt they could do her.

They rode out into the open. Tom's sight was blurred, for last night's drinking had left its mark. But he saw the horse in front of the rock house. He made out a man standing behind the mount. He made out Frio's black hat.

Quayle said, "That him?"

Tom swallowed and looked down. "It's him."

Quayle waved his arm and shouted, "Charge!"

In an instant the troopers were in a gallop. The first rush left Tom behind. He had no wish to be up front. He had no wish to be here at all. He let the soldiers take over. Sick at heart, he watched the fugitive swing into the saddle and spur northward toward the heavy brush.

"Run, Frio!" he found himself whispering. "For God's sake, run!"

Tom touched spurs to his horse then and tried to catch up with Quayle, but already he was too far behind. The troopers hit the brush. The heavy limbs lashed at them, the thorns clutched and tore. But the soldiers had seen their quarry. They spurred through the brush like Mexican vaqueros born to the chaparral. They started a ragged pattern of shooting, but it was of no real avail. There was no chance for accuracy from horseback at a speed like this, through a thorny tangle of brush that grabbed at a man and tried to pull him out of the saddle.

For a mile or more they ran. The horses were

beginning to labor. But the fugitive's mount was slowing more. In despair Tom watched the soldiers making a slow but steady gain. Of a sudden now he wished that by some miracle he could place himself on that horse up yonder, that he could take the soldiers' bullets instead of Frio.

To hell with the major! To hell with the Union! He wished he could call back the day, could have another chance at the decision he had made. Tears burned his eyes and trailed down his cheeks.

"Run, Frio! For God's sake, run!"

The soldiers shouted in excitement. Blinking hard, Tom saw that the quarry's horse had gone down. It lay kicking on the ground. In the brush the fugitive began to run afoot, limping as if the fall had hurt his leg. It occurred to Tom that Frio was making a pretty good account of himself for a man who had been wounded so badly.

Quayle signaled, splitting his riders, sending half of them around one side, half around the other. They would ring Frio and then close in on him. In a few minutes he would be a dead man.

Tom knew the situation was out of his hands now. Nothing he could do would help Frio. He stopped his horse and sat slumped in the saddle, the tears streaming. He wished God would see fit to strike him dead. Oblivion now would be a blessing.

Eyes closed, he could hear the soldiers threshing through the brush. They shouted to one another. Above them all he could hear the loud commands of Major Quayle. Finally came the exultant yells of the men as they cornered their prey.

A volley of shots echoed through the chaparral.

"Frio!" Tom cried. "Oh, God!" He touched spurs to the horse and put him into a run. The choking veil of gunsmoke still clung in the thick brush. Tom spurred past the soldiers toward the still figure he could see lying broken on the ground. He slid his horse to a stop and was off running.

The body lay facedown, torn half apart by the troopers' bullets. Major Quayle rode up and stepped out of the saddle as Tom gently started to turn the body over.

Tom looked into the dirt-covered face and felt his heart bob.

Major Quayle suddenly began to curse. "That's not Wheeler!"

Tom slowly shook his head, his chin dropping. He folded Blas Talamantes's hands carefully and wiped dirt from the Mexican's face. Tears burned in Tom's eyes.

"No, Major," he said tightly, "it's not Frio Wheeler. You've killed the wrong man!"

Frio's wounds burned as if a hot branding iron had been shoved against his shoulder. From its stickiness, he knew it was bleeding afresh. They had carried him here into the thickest of the brush, for he had little strength to support himself. He had leaned heavily upon Amelia and Natividad. María had followed along with Chico. The little woman had a broken-off catclaw limb and was walking backward, scratching out their tracks as she went.

Frio groaned despite himself, for the wound was blindingly painful.

Amelia said, "This is far enough. He'll die if we keep this up." While Natividad held Frio on his feet, Amelia found a thick clump of shoulder-high prickly pear, growing so tightly that at first glance there seemed no way into it. But she found a way and beckoned. "In here. If we'll all huddle in here, they may not find us."

Pear thorns dug into their legs like tiny needles of fire, but there was no time to worry about that now. They moved into the heavy clump. María came last, dragging the catclaw limb to brush away the sign of their passing. It wouldn't fool a good tracker, but it might be overlooked by the Yankees.

"Wrap Frio in this blanket," Amelia said to Natividad. She had taken command with all the firmness of a soldier. "We may have to lie here a long time, and he's going to be cold." They laid him out in a narrow spot between the prickly pears, one edge of the blanket beneath him. Amelia stayed on her feet and watched until the others had bundled themselves and were lying flat upon the ground. Then she crawled under the blanket beside Frio. She found him trembling from cold. She pulled her body against him and drew the blanket up tightly, hoping her own warmth would protect him. With that wound, pneumonia could come easily.

"It's going to be all right, Frio," she whispered.

Presently they heard a far-off volley of shots. María screamed, "Blas! Blas!"

Then came a deadly silence. They could do nothing except lie there and listen to the little woman alternately sobbing and praying. Amelia buried her face against Frio's chest and let her own tears flow.

Much later they heard men and horses approaching slowly. Chico whimpered. María's voice spoke quietly, steady now with resignation, "Easy, little one. Easy, so they do not hear."

The soldiers had fanned out in the brush and were combing it slowly, knowing the man they sought must be hiding there. Amelia turned and lay quietly, her

breath ragged in fear. She knew the cold presence of
death. At ground level was a small opening through
the pear plants, and she could see a Union soldier
moving in her direction. His gaze moved carefully
back and forth. She held her breath, certain he was
going to spot her. She wanted to pull the blanket back
over her face but was afraid the movement would
catch his eye. A scream rose in her throat. She
clamped her teeth together.

The soldier rode close, peering over into this heavy
growth of pear. Amelia's fingers closed on the rifle. If
that trooper saw them, she would shoot him, even
though she knew it would bring the others on the run.
They wouldn't kill Frio without a fight; not without
killing her too!

The soldier saw nothing. He pulled away. Amelia
let her breath out slowly and loosened her hold on the
rifle. Her heart seemed to race.

The line had passed. Unless they came this way
again, Frio was safe.

She saw another movement then. Another rider was
coming, one not in uniform. This man trailed along
behind the soldiers, not taking part in the search.
Amelia squinted, trying to make out his face.

He moved closer, and recognition came with a
shock.

"Tom!" she cried out. Immediately she wanted to
bite off her tongue. Tom McCasland reined up. He had
heard. His gaze searched through the prickly pear, and
their eyes met.

She lay paralyzed in fear, watching her brother, sure
he was going to call back the soldiers.

Then Tom tore his eyes away from her. He dropped
his chin and rode on.

With dusk came the smoke, drifting slowly southward

from the direction of the house. Frio sat up weakly. "They're burnin' us out," he said. A great sadness came over him. He knew Blas was dead.

María stood up, weeping quietly. Frio wished he could go to her.

"María," he said bitterly. "I promise you this: I promise you they'll pay!"

12

For a long time they waited there in the darkness, blankets wrapped tightly around them for warmth. The stars stood out with a piercing brightness in the winter sky. Natividad de la Cruz pushed to his feet, speaking sharply under his breath when his leg brushed against the hostile spines of a prickly pear. "I think, Mr. Frio, the *yanquis* have gone. If you like, I will go see."

Frio nodded painfully. "I doubt they've left us anything to go back to. But go look."

The moon came up while Natividad was gone. Its silver light made the bushes stand out in bold relief. At least, thought Frio, they wouldn't have to stumble along in darkness, pierced by thorns at every wrong step.

He shivered inside the blanket. Amelia McCasland leaned to him, her body pleasantly warm. Another time it might have been different, but her presence brought him little comfort now. Pain pulsed in his shoulder, almost enough to make him cry out. It was as if the bullet were still lodged there with its white heat. Frio knew he would have a fever later. His mind dwelled on Blas Talamantes. He wondered where the Mexican was, wondered if death had come swiftly and with mercy, or if Blas had lain and suffered as Frio suffered now.

Presently they heard brush snapping. Natividad was calling softly. He knew the direction but not the exact place.

Amelia answered, "Here, Natividad."

The Mexican moved cautiously into the big clump of pear, avoiding its thorns. He gazed down gravely at Frio. "Mr. Frio, the *yanqui* soldiers have gone. We can go back to the house if you like." He paused and said, "But, as you say, there is no house."

Amelia looked at Frio, tears in her eyes. Then, squaring her shoulders, she said, "We will go back, Natividad, to whatever is left."

Natividad blinked, not following her reasoning. He shrugged and said, "Of course, señorita. Here, I will help you."

Gently he helped Frio to his feet. The wounded man closed his eyes tightly a moment, shaking his head. His brain seemed to swim aimlessly, and he cringed against a sharp shaft of pain. With Natividad's support, Frio made his way out of the pear.

It took them longer to get back to the clearing than it had taken to reach the pear in the first place. For one thing, there was not the pressure of pursuit. Secondly, there was the dread of seeing what lay in wait for them. Amelia took the lead. María trailed, holding onto Chico's hand. The little woman moved with her head down, but she did not let her grief blind her. She held to the boy, keeping him from walking into thorns, catching him when he stumbled.

Amelia stopped at the edge of the clearing. Frio heard her gasp, "Oh, Frio, oh no!"

Frio blinked, trying to clear the glaze from his eyes. In the moonlight he could see the bare rock walls and the glow from inside them. Though the walls would not burn, they probably were badly cracked from the heat of the blazing roof. The smaller house that Blas and María had used was gone, too, part of one wall caved in, flames still licking hungrily at the wooden beams. The troopers had set fire even to the brush *jacales* that old Salcido Mendoza had built long ago for his vaqueros and their families. The Yankees had not left a thing standing above ground except the corrals and the rock walls.

Anger surged again in Frio Wheeler, a helpless anger that hurt all the more because all he could do was stand here and look. He couldn't even stand were it not for Natividad holding him up.

"We could as well have stayed in the brush," Frio gritted. "We'll have to sleep in the open anyway."

Natividad eased Frio to the ground. Frio sat with his fist balled as tight as he could make it. So many things he could think of now, things they should have done. They should have taken more blankets with them, for the ones they had would not be enough to shield them from the night's cold. They should have taken some food, too, for everything in the houses had been burned. And guns . . . There had been a couple more guns in the bigger house. Chances were the soldiers had found those and confiscated them if they had made any search before they put the place to the torch. Burn them or steal them, it didn't matter much now; the guns were gone. All Frio had was the one rifle.

Natividad gingerly dragged some of the slow-burning wood out of the two houses, careful lest he seàr his hands. He piled it together, then fetched wood from Blas Talamantes's woodpile. Presently he had a fire started between the ruins of the two houses. He said, "We need this tonight, I think."

María had been silent. Now, she asked, "What of Blas?"

Frio said, "Not much anybody can do for him now. Natividad will go look for him in the mornin'."

They spread their blankets near the fire so they would have its warmth through the night. Natividad brought up enough wood to last until day, piling it where he could reach it as it was needed. Chico was the first to drop off in fitful sleep. Before long he was moaning, caught in the clutch of some nightmare.

Sitting close beside Frio, Amelia said, "He was like that for a while after we first came here. Then he got over it. I guess today has brought the scare back to him."

"Poor button," Frio replied. "He must think his saints are almighty angry with him."

María Talamantes leaned over the boy, shaking him a little to try to stir him out of the dream. In Spanish she said, "It's all right, Chico. It's all right." She sat on the ground and took the boy in her arms, folding him to her bosom and rocking her body gently back and forth. Somehow in comforting the boy she seemed to find solace for herself.

Natividad got up and brought his blanket. He put it over the little woman and the boy. He said simply, "With this fire, the blanket is too warm for me." He sat nearer the blaze and gradually dozed off to sleep, his chin dropping to his chest.

For Frio there was little sleep. The fever grew. He

sweated awhile, then chilled. His half-numbed mind slipped off into swirling dreams of violence and movement, to short flights of fancy—some angry, some happy, some frightening, some sad. The faces of Blas Talamantes and Tom McCasland and Florencio Chapa kept coming to him, again and again. He could see his wagons and feel the cold, muddy water of the Rio Grande. He imagined he could hear the guns in far-off Virginia and see the men there low on ammunition, short of guns, waiting for his wagons to bring these things across the river from Mexico. Half-awake, he peered with glazed eyes into the crackling coals of Natividad's fire and saw Brownsville aflame. He could hear the screams of Amelia McCasland, trapped inside the blazing store with her dying father. Another moment he would be back with Tom McCasland in the pleasant years before the war, riding across this ranch, putting their brand on the unclaimed cattle they found. There was no reason to the images he saw, no logical sequence.

He lay until dawn, dozing a little, then half awakening, never a moment free from the torment of his stiffened shoulder. Amelia slept fitfully beside him. With daylight it seemed to him that his fever was gone, and he could see clearly. He watched the sunrise. He saw Natividad reach out to put more wood on the fire, then stand up and stretch himself, his breath making a small patch of fog in the sharp morning air.

Quietly, trying not to awaken the others, the Mexican said to Frio, "There is no food. The boy will be hungry."

They all would be, but it would hurt the boy most of all.

As if in answer, Blas Talamantes's milk cow bawled beside the corral gate. Natividad carefully walked over and opened the gate so she could go in. The cow smelled her way suspiciously up to the ashes of what had been the small brush shed where Blas had been accustomed to milking her. She stood there dumbly and bawled.

Natividad kicked around the ashes of Blas and María's house and found a few blackened pots and pans. He also found a tin bucket. He carried them out to the creek, kneeling to scour the black from them with sand, then washing them clean with water. He held the bucket up to the rising sun to check it for holes. There weren't any. Next he found what was left of a pitchfork, half of the wooden handle burned away. He walked out to the nearest prickly pear and broke off all the spiny pads he could carry. He speared these, several at a time, on the tines of the pitchfork and held them over the fire, burning the thorns away. Done with that, he carried the fire-cleaned pear to the cow and fed it to her. While she chewed, he knelt and milked her.

Returning, he held the bucket up proudly for the awakening women to see. Amelia and María went to the charred remains of the houses and poked around for salvage. They found little. There was no food except the bucket of milk.

Frio said, "Natividad, we are afoot. They must have run off the horses. Can you shoot?"

Natividad shrugged. "Not the best. But maybeso I find us some kind of game."

Frio shook his head. "Not likely, not close to the house. I was thinkin' you might find a cow someplace around, or a steer. Take the rifle and shoot one. We'll have beef anyway. That's a start."

Taking the rifle and the few cartridges, Natividad disappeared into the brush. After a long time they heard two shots. The Mexican returned, his shoulders bent under the weight of a quarter of beef. He said apologetically, "He was not a fat steer, but in the dry time one cannot choose. . . ."

Frio said, "You did fine."

"I will go back and bring more of the beef before the wild hogs find it."

Amelia sand-scoured an iron skillet she had rescued from the ashes. Using tallow from the fresh-killed beef, she soon had beef frying over the coals. By the time Natividad came back with another quarter, Amelia had steak cooked and ready to eat.

Frio drank a little of the warm milk, but he left most of it for María and the boy. What he wanted most was hot coffee. Texans here on the border had been comparatively fortunate in respect to coffee and some of the other imported goods. While the rest of the Confederacy was forced to do without, South Texans continued getting many of these things in limited amounts out of Mexico. But now there would be no coffee for Frio. It had gone up in flames.

Later, a couple of the loose horses came drifting in, for this was home. The Mexican penned them.

"Natividad," Frio said, "I'd be much obliged if you would go out and find Blas. Bring him in so we can bury him decently. Then I'd like you to ride to Matamoros and tell Hugh Plunkett what happened. You ought to be able to smuggle some supplies across the river on pack mules or burros and bring them here."

"Sí, I can do that. But it is not good to leave you here this way. You cannot defend yourself."

Frio shrugged painfully. "What choice do we have? You just hurry. Tell Hugh Plunkett we need help here. He'll find a way to send it."

The Mexican fashioned a hackamore out of some rawhide rope he found. Mounting bareback, he rode off and was gone an hour. When he came back, he was walking, leading the horse. Frio looked away, not wanting to watch. He knew that bundle across the horse's back had to be Blas. María Talamantes arose, crossed herself, and went slowly out to meet Natividad. Then she walked back, moving along dry eyed beside her husband's body.

They wrapped Blas in one of the blankets and buried him in a shallow grave. They placed rocks over him so the wolves would not dig him up. María would not want to leave him here forever. Someday, when she could, she would want to move him to consecrated ground.

There was not even a Bible to read from, for that too had burned. Frio stood on weak legs beside the pile of rocks and recited from memory what he could. María prayed almost inaudibly. When they were done, Natividad de la Cruz mounted the horse bareback and started toward Brownsville.

Frio saw the horseman approaching and thought at first it might be Natividad, coming back for some reason. Frio's sight was still none too good. Soon, though, he could tell it was not Natividad. He pushed painfully to his feet and supported himself against one of the fractured rock walls. "Amelia," he said evenly, "the rifle!"

She quickly handed it to him. With his left arm stiff, he didn't know how he was going to handle it if the need came.

Amelia peered toward the rider and turned back worriedly to Frio. "If it's the Yankees again, you've got to get out of here."

"Where? I've got no strength to run, even if I

wanted to. I ran last night. I'm not ever goin' to run again!"

María came to stand with Amelia and Frio by the smoke-blackened wall. The boy Chico clung to María's skirt. Frio tried in vain to make out some detail about the rider. All he got was a blur. "What does he look like?"

Amelia's mouth dropped open. "It looks like . . ." Her chin came down, and her mouth hardened. "It looks like Tom."

Anger struck Frio. His grip tightened on the rifle. "Reckon he's brought the Yankees with him again?"

Amelia's voice was strained. "I don't see any sign of them." She glanced at Frio's rifle. "Frio, don't do anything in anger. Don't do anything you may regret."

Frio said tightly, "The only thing I regret is that I went through all those years callin' him friend."

Amelia blinked and stopped her tears before they really got started. Gravely she watched Tom McCasland ride in. Tom reined up thirty feet from the ruined house. He started to swing his leg over the saddle.

Frio said sharply, "Stay right where you're at! You're not gettin' off!"

Tom caught himself half out of the saddle. He stopped that way and let his eyes drift over the boy, the two women, and the wounded man who swayed there. Finally he said, "I'm gettin' down. Shoot me if you want to."

Frio raised the rifle, but he found he could not bring his left arm across. If he fired, he would have to do it one-handed. The recoil would probably tear the rifle from his weak grasp.

Frio said, "You got no business here. Get back on that horse."

Tom replied, "Believe me, it took me a long time, workin' up the courage to come back. I'm not leavin' now."

"You got your Yankee friends hidden yonder, someplace in the brush?"

Tom shook his head. "Slipped away from them in the dark. They won't be back, not for a while. They rode half the night, afraid the fires would attract Santos Benavides and his Mexican militia."

Amelia said bitterly. "Why didn't you just keep riding with your Yankees, Tom? There's nobody here who wants you!"

Tom flinched. He stared at her, hurt in his eyes. "I'm still your brother, Amelia."

She shook her head. Her voice was like ice. "I had a brother once. His name was Bert, and he died at Glorieta. There is no other!"

Tom McCasland flexed his hands and looked down at his feet. "I guess I knew how it would be. But I had to come back anyway. I had to try and make you understand how it was . . . why I did it."

She said, "I guess I know why. You've turned Yankee. You've betrayed your family, your friends. . . ."

Tom pointed out, "I could have called them back last night, but I didn't."

Frio put in, "It was too late by then to undo the damage. Blas was already dead."

Tom's gaze went to the slight figure of María Talamantes, and he winced as if in pain. María stared at him with a level, burning gaze. If she had had a rifle in her hands, she probably would have shot him.

"Frio, I had to do it. The confederacy is losin', there's no doubt about that. The question is, how long will it hold on? This border trade helps keep the war goin'. With you gone, the trade would be badly crippled. They made me see that it was your life against the thousands who might be saved if the war was cut a little shorter. It was a bitter choice, but I had to do it." Tom clenched his fists and said, "Now I've told you why I came. If you want to use that rifle, just go ahead."

Frio's hand tightened, but the rifle didn't fire. He asked, "How come you changed your mind last night? Why didn't you call the troops back?"

Tom shook his head. "I can't rightly say. Lost my nerve, I guess. All of a sudden those thousands of men didn't seem real to me. But *you* were real, Frio. You were my friend."

Frio's voice was harsh. "Friend? All these years Blas Talamantes was the best friend I had, and I didn't have sense enough to see it till he died to save me." He raised the muzzle of the rifle. "Now get back on that horse, Tom. If Amelia wasn't here—if she wasn't your sister—I'd kill you where you stand. As it is, I'll let you go." His eyes narrowed. "But one day we'll meet and she won't be there. When that day comes, Tom, I'm goin' to kill you!"

The gray look of defeat was in Tom's face. He swung onto the horse. To María he said, "I'm sorry. I wish it had been me instead of Blas."

He glanced once more in despair at Frio and Amelia. Then he turned the horse around and rode away.

13

WITH A RAW NORTH wind lashing against the end-gates, the groaning wagons toiled through deep sand, mules straining against the harness. On the wagons, teamsters with serapes pulled up around their ears cracked whips and shouted at the mules to pull harder.

Down from the point of the wagon train came the rider, tall and gaunt, black whiskers grayed by trail dust, eyes steeled against the constant company of raw hurt. He rode with left arm hanging stiff at his side, his heavy coat bulky with the thickness of a bandage wrapped around his shoulder. He paused at every wagon, his face dark as a storm cloud.

"Keep 'em movin'! Don't let 'em hold back on you! We got to make the well before dark!"

He rode hunched, for every step the horse took drove a thin shaft of pain through Frio Wheeler's shoulder. But he never held back. He had worn out two horses already today, moving up and down this line like some grim, avenging demon, roaring orders, driving, threatening. His face had thinned. Dark hollows had dug in under his eyes. And the eyes themselves had something burning in them that made a man instinctively step aside. No one had seen him smile in weeks now. He had always been a firm man when it came to the wagons, but now he had gone beyond firmness. Not a man on the train was immune from the sharp lash of his angry voice.

He had been like this ever since he had caught up to his wagons on their way down from San Antonio, Happy Jack Fleet in charge. Frio had been a changed man. A couple of the more superstitious among his Mexican teamsters had speculated aloud if perhaps Satan himself had cast a spell upon *el patrón*. Perhaps the real Frio had died, and *El Diablo* had placed some malevolent spirit in his body to walk among men and do evil.

The Devil himself could not have driven the men much harder than Frio was doing. He had taken his last shipment of cotton by way of Rio Grande City and down to Matamoros in a day and a half less than any other freighter on the road. He had made the return trip with a cargo of English rifles, bar lead, powder, and mercury in two days less than anyone else. Now, this trip, it looked as if he was determined to shave time even from his own record.

"Patrón," one of the teamsters argued, "this team, she is get very tired."

"They'll pull if you crack that whip!"

Frio finally reached the rear wagon, his throat raw from dust and shouting. Happy Jack rode there, his solemn, appraising eyes mirroring his quiet disapproval.

Frio ignored the cowboy's unspoken but obvious opinion. "Damn it, Happy, can't you keep these rear wagons pushed up? Way this train is all strung out, we'll be the middle of next summer gettin' to Matamoros."

Happy met Frio's hard gaze without giving any ground. "Way we're goin' we won't get there at all. You're fixin' to have a bunch of dead mules on your hands. Maybe some dead *mulateros* too."

"The faster we move, the more trips we can make. We're doin' it for the Confederacy."

Happy's mouth turned down. "A mule, he don't know nothin' about war. He only knows when he's wore out. You can't talk much patriotism to a mule."

"They'll get their rest."

"When? That's what you said the last trip, but they didn't get any."

Frio snapped. "If you don't like the way I run these wagons, why don't you just leave?"

Happy's eyes reflected a quick anger, which he just as quickly shoved aside. "Because I know it's that shoulder that makes you so damn mean, and I keep rememberin' how you come to get that bullet in you. You thought I was in trouble, and you went to get me out."

Frio wished he hadn't spoken so sharply. If it weren't for this shoulder. . . . "I'd have done it for any man on the train."

"The point is, you did it for *me*. So I reckon I'll stay on till you kill me. But you're apt to kill yourself first, the pace you're keepin'." He frowned. "You ought to've listened to that doctor in San Antonio. He said you needed to be on your back instead of in the saddle. That shoulder still hurts you somethin' fierce, don't it?"

Frio didn't look him in the eye. "I hadn't noticed."

"You're a liar. You was more dead than alive when you caught up to us and took over the train. You ain't much better even yet. You're so bad poisoned that if a rattlesnake was to bite you, he'd die."

Frio lifted his right hand and gripped the left shoulder, his face twisting. "I know I been ridin' all of you pretty hard. Had a lot on my mind."

"You can't win the war all by yourself."

Frio lowered his hand, the fist knotted. "But I want them to know I'm still alive. I want them to know that they not only didn't stop me, they made me work harder than I ever worked before. I want them to stand there by the river and count those cotton bales and curse the day they sent that patrol out to kill me."

"That's how you're takin' your revenge, puttin' more bales across the river?"

Frio's clenched teeth gleamed white against the black of his whiskers as he stared south. "For now, Happy. For now."

Riding at the head of the line, Frio kept his sharp gaze sweeping along the fringe of brush, watching for anything that didn't belong—any movement, any patch of color. He didn't believe for a moment that the Yankees had given up on killing him. Way up front this way, he would make a prime target for any sharpshooter lurking out yonder. From the bushwhacker's viewpoint, though, it would be a risky proposition. Even though he could bring Frio down with an easy shot, the train's outriders and Happy Jack would go into immediate pursuit. Anyone who fired on Frio would be committing suicide.

Frio figured it would take a deep loyalty to the Union, a deep hatred for him personally, or a big offer of money to persuade a man to take that kind of assignment.

Happy Jack's quiet protest had forced Frio to recognize something he hadn't wanted to see. The mules *were* wearing out, and the teamsters weren't much better off. He *had* been driving them too hard. He knew his anger and hatred had given him a desperate strength and a dogged determination he couldn't expect the other men to share.

It was almost dark when he sighted the well he had been aiming for. He saw three men standing beside it, holding horses. His right hand tightened on the saddle-gun that lay across his lap, but he kept riding. From a distance he could tell that all three were Mexicans. Close in, he recognized one as a militiaman he had seen in Rio Grande City. The others would be too. Their old clothes had worn ragged, and the men looked hungry. The Confederacy had been woefully slow in paying its militia, especially down here on the river, so far from the seat of government.

With typical Mexican exaggerated deference toward an Anglo, the ranking one of the three stepped forward, sombrero in hand. "Señor Wheeler, we have wait for you. I am Pablo Lujan. These are Aparicio Jiminez and Lupe Martín."

Frio brought himself stiffly down from the saddle, his face contorted until the shock of movement was past. He extended his hand. "I know you, Pablo. You're with Colonel Benavides, aren't you?"

"*Sí*, we make a little patrol, these vaqueros and me. Long time ago we hunt stray cattle. Now we hunt stray *yanquis*. You see any?"

Frio shook his head. "It's been as peaceful as the inside of the Matamoros church, all the way down from San Antonio. You got trouble on this end?"

Pablo Lujan, nodding gravely, swept one hand in the direction of the brush. "There is sign. The *yanquis*, they have soldiers somewhere in the *bosque*. Some soldiers that are soldiers and some that are *not* soldiers."

"Irregulars?"

"*Sí*, that is the word. They put a blue uniform on some of the *renegados* and call them soldiers. But they are still only *renegados*. They know how to find water, which the *yanqui* does not. They know where to look for the wagon trains, which the *yanqui* does not."

Frio frowned, "It's nothin' new for the Yankees to hire outlaws and call them legal. They've done it right along."

Lujan shrugged. "In their place, señor, would we not do the same? Even in Colonel Benavides's company there are some among us who could never be priests."

Frio's mouth went aslant as he caught the humor in the Mexican's eyes. Frio didn't laugh, but he felt better for this encounter at the waterhole. He had always admired the simple, unquestioning logic of the Mexicans. They were a straightforward people in many ways, philosophically accepting life's many contradictions. He liked their logic even when he couldn't accept it for himself.

"What other news do you hear on the border?" Frio asked.

"We hear the Rip Ford is come pretty soon from San Antonio with many men to drive the *yanquis* back into the sea. Do you think this is true?"

Frio nodded. "I haven't seen him. I've only heard the rumors. But I expect it's true."

"We hear he has ten thousand men."

Frio shook his head. "*One* thousand would be more

like it. Texas couldn't even feed ten thousand." It was always a mystery to him how rumors could magnify so much in war. They grew faster than a bunch of cotton-tail rabbits. Just such wild rumor as this had scared the Confederate General Bee into leaving Brownsville so precipitously.

But maybe this time rumor could play against the Yankees. If they had heard the same ten-thousand-man report as these Mexican militiamen, they were proba-bly getting nervous now in Fort Brown. And Rip Ford was a shrewd soldier. Maybe he had fostered the rumor himself.

Frio said to Lujan, "Keep tellin' everybody it's ten thousand. Old Rip may have the battle won before it starts."

He looked back at his wagons, which were circling for a night's camp near the well. "Pablo, we'd be tickled if you boys would stay and eat with us tonight."

Lujan smiled. "What for do you think we wait here, Señor Wheeler? The militiaman must live off the land, and in this dry time the land is very poor. Some-times, when God blesses us, we can eat with the wagons."

It was well after dark when the mules had been watered and fed and the teamsters could settle down for supper. Frio had no appetite and took little food into his plate. He picked around on it, not eating half. Mostly he drank coffee, black and steaming.

Happy Jack's appetite had suffered none. He fin-ished a second helping of beef and beans and set his tin plate down on the bare ground beside him. He watched Frio sipping strong black coffee. "Frio," he said, "you're not goin' to get any weller till you start eatin' again. You don't eat nothin', just drink coffee and smoke cigarettes. You don't get half a night's sleep, either. You just pace around camp in the dark like a bobcat in a box."

"Shoulder like this, a man can't sleep much. As for food, who can eat much at such a time?"

Happy said, "I can." He pointed his chin toward the three Mexican militiamen, who were scraping up all the leavings, letting nothing go to waste. "Don't seem like dark times has hurt their appetite much, either. Them poor boys was hungry."

Frio grimaced, watching the three. "It's a long way to Austin, and a longer way yet to Richmond. Easy for the government to forget a handful of men down here on the border. But if it wasn't for Benavides and his militia, the Yankees would have the Rio Grande plumb to Laredo and Eagle Pass. There wouldn't be any border trade."

Happy nodded. "They're poor devils with their bellies half empty and the pants hangin' off of their seat. But we owe them a lot."

They sat awhile in silence. Frio stared into the dwindling fire, his mind wandering aimlessly down a dozen different trails. Happy brooded, chewing his lip. Frio began to notice, for it wasn't like Happy to worry much.

"You got somethin' on your mind, Happy?"

Happy shrugged. "Been worryin'. Guess I caught that from you, like some contagious sickness. Probably just foolishness anyway." His eyes met Frio's a minute. "Did you notice anything unusual today?"

"How do you mean?"

"I don't know. Didn't really see nothin', just kind of felt it. Had the feelin' somebody was out in that brush watchin' us. Trailin' along."

"How come you didn't tell me?"

"Because like I said, I didn't see nothin'. Just a feelin', a foolish notion, maybe. Way you been lately, you'd make anybody a little jumpy." Happy waited for some reply and didn't get it. "You haven't said anything, Frio. You think I'm just lettin' my imagination run wild?"

Frio shook his head and came as near smiling as he had in weeks. "No, Happy. I just think you're finally gettin' some idea of what a man has to suffer through when he's an owner."

It was a chilly night, the stars icy crystals sparkling against a black sky. Frio huddled by the fire, gazing into the coals, remembering. It seemed he was doing a lot of that lately during the long nights when he was unable to sleep, and when he was too tired or in too much pain to stalk around camp worrying the guards. He thought back on how he had left Amelia Mc-Casland at the ranch.

He hadn't wanted to do it. When Natividad de la Cruz had returned with a wagonload of contraband supplies and a couple of men Hugh Plunkett had sent, Frio had tried to talk Amelia into taking María and Chico back to either Brownsville or Matamoros.

"There's nothin' left out here for you now," he had said, pointing to the charred ruins. "Not even a roof over your heads."

"We've got help," Amelia had answered. "We can put up a brush *jacal*. It'll be enough to keep us warm and dry."

"You've got no guarantee the Yankees won't come back and try again. Anything we build, they'll burn down."

"Then we'll build another, and another. You said you were through running, Frio. So am I. I've made up my mind: Right here is where I'm going to stay."

Frio had known enough stubborn people to recognize the signs. He knew there was no point in arguing with her. So he had the three Mexicans put up a pair of rude brush huts, one for the two women and the boy, the other for Natividad. De la Cruz was to stay and do what he could to keep the ranch together. That wouldn't be much, Frio had feared, for you didn't find many men like Blas Talamantes. Still, Natividad would try, and he would be some protection for the women. Maybe when this war was over there would still be enough of the cattle left so that Frio could start fresh and rebuild.

As soon as he could stay on a horse, Frio had told Amelia he was going to rejoin the wagon train. She had nodded in resignation and made no protest, for she knew something of stubborn people too.

She said, "You told me that the next time you went to Matamoros you would take me along. You said you wanted to marry me."

Frio had not tried to look into her eyes. "I did, and I meant it. But things have changed now, Amelia. When Tom led the Yankees out here and shot Blas, that altered everything. One day I'll have to kill him. You might not want to be married to me then."

Amelia had said tightly, "Do you really have that much hate in you, Frio?"

Frio had reached up to touch his bad shoulder and said, "I reckon I do."

"Go then," Amelia told him. "Do whatever you have to. When it's over, I'll still be here."

The fire had burned low. One of the teamsters brought an armload of dead brush and dropped it near the glowing coals. "*Con permiso, patrón,* I will build up the fire."

Frio pushed himself to his feet and backed away a step. "Go ahead."

The Mexican began to lay wood on the smoldering fire. Flames started to build, licking around the dry mesquite and catclaw limbs. The dancing light brightened, framing Frio and the teamster against the darkness.

Frio saw a flash from out in the brush and at almost the same instant felt an angry tug at the sleeve of his coat. Unprepared, he staggered backward in surprise. His foot caught on the little pile of wood, and he fell just as the rifle crashed again. Later he knew that this fall had saved his life, for the bullet thumped into the sideboard of a wagon behind him. The fall jarred the wounded shoulder, and a paralyzing agony gripped him.

But if Frio was caught unprepared, Happy Jack and the Benavides militiamen were not. Almost as soon as Frio went down, he heard four more guns open up, aimed at the last flash from the darkness. The ambusher fired a third time, and the camp rifles roared again.

Out in the brush a man screamed. Still lying on his side, the shoulder throbbing, Frio heard a crackling of dry limbs in the darkness. Guns in hand, Happy and the three militiamen sprinted out toward the bush-whacker, half a dozen teamsters close behind them. Frio heard one of the militiamen cry out sharply in Spanish, "Do not touch that gun!"

The reply was a weak cry for mercy. Presently the militiamen came back into the firelight, carrying a wounded man. Frio had regained his feet, although he was shaking a little from surprise and pain. They laid the wounded man down by the fire. Happy returned, still looking off into the darkness. "Far as I can tell, he was by himself."

The ambusher was Mexican, and he was dying. Frio could not remember ever having seen the hombre before. In Spanish he asked, "What did you do this for? Did the *yanquis* pay you?"

The Mexican's teeth grated in agony. He shook his head. "Not the *yanquis* . . . Florencio Chapa. He said he would pay . . ." The man cried out in pain. Shock covered his face with cold sweat. He would be dead in a minute. "Chapa said he would give me . . . much silver . . . to kill the man Wheeler . . . for the terrible thing he has done to Chapa."

"For what I did to *him*?" Frio said sharply.

"You have not seen him," came the weak reply. "Few have seen him since . . ." The man groaned as the pain grew more intense. "It is a terrible sight . . . a terrible sight. . . ." The voice trailed, and he was gone.

Happy Jack stood solemnly staring down on the ambusher he had helped to kill. At last he looked up at Frio. "Appears you've got more enemies than the law allows. I'm still glad I'm not an owner!"

14

SPRING. DROUGHT STILL CLUNG stubbornly to the land. The brush leafed out green, for this was desert growth that had survived similar droughts periodically for thousands of years and had met Nature's strict law of selectivity. The plants that couldn't survive had died out in times so remote as to be beyond the memory of man.

Except for those scattered spots that had been fortunate in receiving the small spotted showers so characteristic of Texas droughts, there was no grass. It would appear to have died out. But Frio knew from past experience that it was merely dormant, waiting for rain to bring it springing fresh and green from bare ground.

The drought worked severe hardship on Frio and the other freighters who moved their wagons ever so slowly along the twisting trails from San Antonio to the Rio Grande and then down to Matamoros. They

still had to carry feed for the mules, and this took up
space that otherwise could have been devoted to cargo.
In that respect the Mexican outfits with their ox teams
and high-wheeled *carretas* had an advantage. They
would make the oxen live largely off prickly pear, the
thorns burned away. But the mule teams were still the
fastest. Frio figured what he lost in carrying capacity
he made up for in time.

There was a consolation. If the drought was hard on
these men who rode the long trails for the Confederacy, it was far harder on the bluecoats who ventured
out on horseback from the rebuilt gates of Fort Brown.
Even with the Texas Unionists they had enlisted, the
federals had not overcome the disadvantage of being
strangers to the land. After all these months, they were
still tied largely to the river. They could not stray farther from it than the water supplies they carried would
allow. Moreover, the near-dry Rio Grande prevented
them from making effective tactical use of the
steamers. Had the river been flowing full, the big
boats, bristling with Yankee guns, might have penetrated upriver past Reynosa and Rio Grande City to
Mier, that bloody-historied town with a name still
black as sin in the remembering eyes of Texas.

Frio rode straight in the saddle again. The pain was
gone, and only a trace of stiffness remained in his left
shoulder. He could use the arm for almost anything
except heavy lifting. He had plenty of men to do that
for him. Though still spare from constant riding, he no
longer had that gaunt look that he had carried so long.
He seldom smiled, but he was no longer a terror to the
men who rode alongside him. They could talk with
him man to man, and he would stop to listen. He knew
when the teams were tired and needed rest. He still

made good time on the trail, but he didn't kill men and mules to do it.

Leaving San Antonio on this trip, Frio had heard news that did more for his spirit than any amount of medicine: At last Rip Ford was about to head south. This forceful Confederate officer would have a good command with him—tough soldiers, expert horsemen. No one knew exactly when Ford was going to start or what route he would take. That was being kept secret. That he was going to move, though, was no secret. Ford wanted the federals to know it. He wanted the new General Herron in Fort Brown to sit and brood over it, as Confederate officers had brooded about the Union's coming.

Ford's campaign would be waged with nerves as much as with guns.

Here on the wheel-rutted trails of the *algodones*, stray units of bold federal soldiers had been fighting their own war of nerves. With them rode attached irregulars—mostly *renegados*—to strike sporadically at the wagon trains. The raids were scattered and completely unpredictable. Usually the riders set fire to as many wagons as they could, then faded back into the chaparral. This they had learned from their enemy Benavides. If they met determined opposition, they most often melted away and saved their strength to use against some weaker train.

Two abortive attempts had been made against Frio's wagons. Both times the Yankees had drawn back quickly, recognizing that Frio's train was too big for them, his men too ready to fight. Frio had drilled his men like soldiers in the art of defense.

He would have admitted that these federals showed good sense. They knew when to strike and when to run.

Today something was wrong. He had smelled it from the beginning, and a vague uneasiness had plagued him all day. This morning he had met a pair of Texas-Mexican militiamen on the trail. They had told him Benavides had gone upriver to head off a detail of bluecoats who somehow had penetrated beyond Rio Grande City and were a threat to the western trails. Later in the day Frio had spied a horseman sitting far off in the distance, watching the train across a clearing in the brush. He had sent one of his outriders to investigate, but the man had faded away before the outrider came close to him.

A Union spy, Frio had been sure. Somewhere out here there must be a Union striking force, or there would have been no need for a spy. He had deployed the outriders and had ordered Happy Jack to fall well behind and watch for any sign of attack from the rear. This way the train probably could be warned in time to circle up for a fight.

At the midday rest, Happy Jack had ridden in unhappily, looking back over his shoulder. "Frio, I seen a man while ago. He was just a-sittin' there on his horse, watchin' me from a couple or three hundred yards. I turned to ride in his direction and he just sort of melted. He was there one minute, then gone the next, hidden in all that brush."

Frio had handed the young man a cup of coffee and watched him take it as eagerly as if it had been whisky. "Did he have a uniform on?"

Happy Jack shook his head. "No, his clothes was Mexican, and so was the riggin'. Kind of a fancy outfit, seemed like at the distance." He looked up, his eyes solemn. "Frio, I never did get close enough to be sure, but just by the way he sat there, the way he looked, I'd swear and be damned that it was Florencio Chapa!"

A chill passed through Frio. He touched the nearly healed shoulder with his hand. "Chapa wouldn't be out here by his lonesome."

Happy Jack frowned and flipped the dregs out of the cup. "No sir, he wouldn't. I'll bet you a pretty that he's got him some *bandidos* waitin' out yonder. Or he's spyin' for a bunch of Yankees and hopin' to see them kill you too dead to skin."

The chill came again. Something strange had developed about Chapa. From talk Frio had heard last time he was in Matamoros, nobody ever saw the *bandido* anymore. Oh, he seemed to be around, all right; he left his tracks. But he was keeping himself out of sight. What business he had in town, he sent someone else to do, sometimes the gringo Campsey, sometimes his own Mexican lieutenants.

There was trembling talk of a masked Chapa, riding through the dark streets of Matamoros at night, evil as a black wolf and hiding his face from the world. Some of the Mexican people were sure Chapa had been revealed as an incarnation of the devil, that his presence had become a curse upon the land where he walked, that if he took off his boots his feet would leave a cloven track and nothing would ever grow there again.

Frio had never counted himself a superstitious man, but when a man lived among people who were prone to superstition, some of it was bound to rub off on him. Sometimes he could almost feel the presence of Chapa. It was an eerie sensation, a malevolent presence that made the hair stiffen on the back of his neck.

"Well," he said to Happy, "if it *was* Chapa, I expect we'll hear from him soon enough. We're coverin' mostly open country this afternoon. I'll string the wagons out two abreast and keep them closed up."

Happy Jack quietly ate his dinner, his eyes on Frio most of the time. Finished, he put away his plate and said with a gravity that was rare in him: "Frio, you're an owner, and it ain't my place to be tellin' you what to do. But I'd give you a little advice: Let me ride out front and you stay up close to these wagons. If it is Chapa, and he gets you cut off from the bunch, he'll take you like a hawk takes a pullet. Won't be enough left of you to even hold a funeral."

Frio placed his hand on Happy Jack's shoulder. "Thanks, Happy. But I never ask anybody to do anything for me that I wouldn't do myself. I'll take the point same as I always do." Happy's eyes showed the young man's worry. Frio added: "I promise you this, I'll see everything that moves. I won't miss even a jackrabbit."

Frio took the point when the wagons strung out again. Gradually the brush thinned and the country opened up. Seeing less chance of being cut off unawares, he began gradually easing farther and farther out in front, the saddlegun across his lap, ready to use.

Moving along at the wagons' pace, he let himself think of Amelia McCasland, riding the ranges herself now like any cowboy, supervising Natividad de la Cruz and a couple of other vaqueros Frio had managed to find across the river. María Talamantes, her time no longer far away, was doing most of the woman work around the place. Amelia was busy a-horseback, seeing that Frio's brand was burned on every unclaimed, unmarked animal she came across. There were a lot of them, for the hard winter had caused untold thousands of cattle to drift southward across the Wild Horse

Desert from drought-stricken ranges above. Many had died of starvation, but a great number had somehow survived, gaunt and shaggy specimens of brute endurance that had survived by eating prickly pear—thorns and all. They were scattered from the Nueces to the Rio Grande, waiting to be claimed by whoever had the fastest horses and the longest ropes.

They hadn't married yet, she and Frio. There hadn't been time. But whenever Amelia spoke, it was always *we* or *us*, and Frio liked the sound of it. "We're going to come out of this thing standing on both feet, Frio," she had told him the last time he had seen her. "Nobody but God will ever know who all those cattle belong to, and He will give them to the one who claims them. They're going to be ours, as many of them as the vaqueros and I can brand."

A couple of times Yankee patrols had stopped at the ranch, hoping to catch Frio there. On both occasions they had started to burn the new brush *jacales*, but Amelia's stubborn defiance had stopped them cold.

Frio remembered wondering, a long time ago, if she was strong enough to be a rancher's wife in this backward country. The thought was ridiculous to him now. Amelia McCasland had a will of iron.

Frio saw the one man first. Stopping his horse, he reached into his saddlebag for the spyglass he always carried. It wasn't enough to bring the man up sharply. Frio couldn't recognize him. But that chill played up and down his back. Instinct told him this was Chapa. Lowering the spyglass and looking around, he saw dust farther to the right. He focused the glass on that and made out riders, coming up from the south. Sunlight touched something metal. A saber, likely.

Frio reined the horse around and put the spurs to

him. Running hard, he drew his pistol and fired it twice, into the air. He waved his hat in a circular motion over his head. The teamsters in the lead saw him. They were already circling the wagons when he got there.

The Mexicans cracked their whips, shouted excitedly at the mules as they moved into their allotted places and drew the wagons up close for a defense. Jumping down, they freed the mules from the wagons but left them in harness. A narrow space remained between the last two wagons so the outriders could come through. Shouting, moving in a hurry and stirring lots of dust, the teamsters tumbled cotton bales down from the wagons and dragged them into line to serve as a breastworks.

Happy Jack was the last man into the circle, bringing up the rear. He jumped to the ground, saddle-gun in hand, and turned his horse loose in the middle. Three men dragged a cotton bale into place to plug the gap. Happy had seen the dust of the approaching riders.

"Yankees?" he demanded of Frio.

"I didn't ask to see their papers."

Happy glanced over the preparations that had been made in a matter of minutes. He whistled his approval. "Say, Frio, if this here war lasts another three years, them *mulateros* are goin' to learn."

"They've learned a right smart already. It'll be a tough outfit that whips this bunch now."

Happy's grin faded as he watched the dust. "Them yonder may be just the outfit that can do it. Jehoso-phat, how many are they?"

Frio's mouth went dry. The dust was still too thick to allow him any sort of count. A hundred cavalrymen, at least. Maybe twice that many.

Seeing they had no surprise, the federals moved up boldly. They could tell the wagon train was prepared for a fight. Frio watched the commanding officer raise his hand and stop the men two hundred yards away. For a minute or two there was movement back and forth in front of the formation, a huddle of half a dozen riders. Presently one man moved out alone, approaching the wagon train. He held up a rifle with a large white handkerchief tied to the barrel.

Frio saw a couple of his teamsters leveling on the man. "It's a flag of truce," he called. "Don't anybody shoot."

He stepped between two wagons and watched the horseman approach in a leisurely walk. Frio squinted, wishing he had the glass with him so he could make the man out. He could tell the rider was a civilian, not in uniform.

Suddenly Frio spat. "I might've known it. That's Tom McCasland!"

Frio waited until Tom neared the circle of wagons, then he moved out into view, the saddlegun in his hand. Tom stopped his horse ten feet away and looked down at him, a light breeze picking up the white flag and waving it. The breeze carried a strong smell of dust.

"Howdy," he said evenly.

"Tom." Frio's voice was hostile.

"Been a while since I saw you last, Frio. How's the shoulder?"

"Good enough that I don't have to crawl through the brush anymore when the Yankees come."

"Mind if I get down?"

"Do what suits you."

Tom swung to the ground and stretched his legs. "Sure tired," he said. "Been a long ride."

"You could've saved it. You're not goin' to get anything here."

Tom allowed himself a long, silent look at the circle of wagons, and at the teamsters who knelt purposefully behind the downed cotton bales, each one with a rifle in his hands. Tom said, "I'll admit I didn't expect to find you'd been drillin' these men in military defense. I thought you were only freightin'."

"Everybody has got to be a soldier of sorts these days."

Tom's eyes were solemn as they cut back to Frio. "Of sorts, but that's all. Those men out yonder"—he pointed his thumb toward the Yankee troopers— "they're *real* soldiers, trained for this kind of thing. Frio, we came to stop your wagon train."

Frio's mouth was grim, but he made no answer.

Tom said, "We *will* stop you, Frio. How we do it is up to you." He swept his hand toward the soldiers. "We've got upward of two hundred and fifty men yonder. All well armed and well mounted. How many men have you got in here? Fifty at the outside. We've got you outnumbered by five to one." He cast a critical eye at the teamsters he could see peering over the bales. "And I'd say we've got you outgunned too, man for man. My experience is that most Mexican teamsters can't shoot."

Frio said tightly, "You can find out mighty quick."

"Give up, Frio. It'd be better all around. In any case, we're not leavin' here till we've taken these wagons. Give up now and there won't be any blood spilled. Not by your men and not by those out yonder."

Frio frowned, one eye almost shut. "Sayin' I agreed, what would you do to my men?"

"Nobody would get hurt. Those from Mexico would be sent home on parole. The others—you included—

would simply be detained until the war is over. Way it's goin', that shouldn't be too long anymore."

"And the wagons?"

"We'll have to burn them." He watched Frio's face. "I'm sorry about this, Frio. I know you've got a lot of money tied up in this outfit. That's somethin' we can't help. You can see for yourself, we have to burn them."

Anger began to churn in Frio. "What does Florencio Chapa get out of it?"

Tom's eyes widened in surprise. "Chapa? He's got nothin' to do with it."

Derisively Frio said, "Don't tell me you've gotten too much religion to ride with Chapa anymore."

"The Union washed its hands of Chapa when he tried to torture you. The government doesn't countenance that sort of thing, even in war."

Frio pointed to a figure sitting on a horse, far off at the edge of the chaparral. "Then what's he doin' there?"

Tom turned quickly, mouth open in surprise. "That can't be Chapa!"

"It is. We been seein' him off and on all day."

In disbelief Tom said, "But we haven't seen him since . . ." He broke off, understanding suddenly coming into his face. "We hired some Mexican scouts who offered to spy out your wagon train for us. We had no idea Chapa was behind them."

Frio snorted. "You expect me to believe that, Tom, after all you've done? Promisin' nothin' would happen to us if we give ourselves up to you. . . . I'll bet you got a deal with Chapa to turn us over to him for his help. *Me*, anyway."

"No, Frio, I swear we don't!"

"Then what's he doin', hangin' around out there like a buzzard?"

Tom shook his head, completely at a loss. "He hates you, Frio. Maybe he just wants to watch us destroy you."

Frio stared hard at Tom McCasland, his eyes narrowed. He found himself wanting to believe Tom. It didn't seem likely that Tom was renegade enough to turn him over to Chapa. Not on purpose. But maybe Chapa had some idea for getting his hands on Frio anyway. . . .

Frio saw a movement off to the north, out of Tom's range of view. A rider was coming fast, pushing his horse as hard as it could go.

Tom said, "The major gave me ten minutes to talk with you, Frio. Time's playin' out."

Frio's eyes were still on the horseman. For some reason he felt a fresh surge of hope. He would play for time—all the time he could delay. "You won't get away with this, Tom. For all you know, Santos Benavides may be comin' right now. Those Yankees of yours are no match for him."

Tom shook his head. "No luck, Frio. We sent a small force to lure Benavides west. He won't be around to help you."

Still unseen by Tom, and unheard because of the rattle of harness and chain and the movement of the mules inside the circle, the horseman rode straight toward the Union column. Frio watched the man slide to a stop in front of the federals. Pandemonium struck among the blue-clad troopers. The half dozen men at the head of the column milled indecisively, looking north.

Frio glanced north and saw a column of dust rising, uptrail.

The federals began turning their horses around. In a moment they were in retreat, moving south. One

Union officer remained momentarily, waving his hat at Tom and shouting. But Tom's back was turned to him, and the officer's voice, along with the sound of retreat, was lost in the noise closer at hand.

Frio watched without expression until he saw the officer give up and pull away, afraid to come any nearer for the time he would lose.

Tom said, "Time's up, Frio. What's it goin' to be?"

A harsh smile broke across Frio's face. "Maybe you better take a look behind you. Then you tell *me*."

Tom turned. The color left him momentarily as he saw that he had been abandoned. He turned back and found that Frio had raised the muzzle of the saddle-gun. It was pointed at Tom's chest. Frio said triumphantly, "There's a cloud of dust in the north yonder. Maybe that's what made those good friends of yours ride off and dump you in our lap."

Tom saw the dust. Disbelief was in his eyes. "It can't be Benavides. The spies told us. . . ."

Frio said, "The spies were wrong. Unless . . ." The idea hit him suddenly, and he felt an elation he hadn't known in months. "Rip Ford!" he exclaimed. "Bound to be! Rip Ford and his column, comin' south to retake the border!"

Tom still held the rifle in one hand, the white handkerchief tied to the barrel. The weapon was empty, but it would have done him no good now if it had been loaded. He dropped it. Shrugging, he said with a fatalism he had learned from the Mexicans, "So now we've swapped places, Frio. 'While ago I was givin' you my terms. Now you can give me yours."

Frio nodded grimly. "That time after they shot Blas, I told you I'd kill you one day."

Tom swallowed. "I remember. So now's your

chance. Do it and get it over with." He squared his shoulders.

Frio studied him awhile, his hands tight on the rifle. "With you just standin' there helpless? That may be the Yankee way of doin'. It's not mine."

"You want to give me a gun and us two shoot it out?"

"I'd rather do it that way than this."

Tom shook his head. "I raised my hand against you once, Frio. I won't do it again, not this way."

Frio lowered the muzzle a little. "Then I reckon we'll just have to hold you and turn you over to the Confederacy."

Tom nodded soberly. "They'll kill me for you, and your hands will stay clean, is that it? You know they'll hang me."

Frio hadn't had time to consider that. The thought shook him. "Don't you think you've earned it?"

"By your lights, I suppose I have."

"Not by yours?"

"I did my duty as I saw it. It was bitter sometimes, but I did my duty the way you did yours. I don't want to hang, Frio. That's no fit way for a man to die."

Frio just stared at him, uncertain what to do.

Tom glanced toward the approaching dust. "Frio, if you want me dead, then for God's sake be man enough to shoot me! Don't leave me to hang!"

Frio still stood there trying to decide, his mouth dry and bitter. Once he might have squeezed the trigger without a qualm. Now, holding the power of death in his hand, he could not move. What he had taken for hatred against Tom he knew now had been a deep hurt, and a vengeful anger. Here, in the face of this mortal test, anger drained away. His hands trembled. His stomach suddenly went cold with the realization of what he might have done.

He stared into the anxious face of Tom McCasland and tried to find there the look of an enemy. Instead, despite all that had come between them, he saw only the face of an old friend.

He lowered the saddlegun. "You came under a flag of truce, Tom. I'll honor that. Now get on your horse and clear out of here, fast."

Tom's eyes were wide, as if he was afraid he hadn't heard right.

Frio said simply, "Damn it, man, I said get on that horse and ride!" He glanced toward the dust. He could almost make out the individual riders. "Don't go south after them Yankees. Ford's men'll catch you. Go west into the brush. Drop south later and swim the Rio."

Tom swung into the saddle. His horse sensed the excitement and began to prance, wanting to run. Tom held the reins up tight. "What are you doin' this for, Frio?"

Frio shouted, "How the hell do I know?" He reached down and picked up Tom's empty rifle with the handkerchief tied to it. He pitched it to him. *"Ándele!"*

Tom skirted the circled wagons and moved into a lope, heading toward the nearest brush. That was to the west. Frio stood slump shouldered and watched him disappear.

Happy Jack Fleet moved up beside Frio to watch the dust-veiled horsemen coming out of the north. "Frio, you done the right thing."

Frio shook his head. "I don't know, Happy. I swear, I just don't know."

The vanguard of the Texas column rode up in a lope, dust an impenetrable fog behind it. Only the two officers at the head of the group wore what could be recognized as a Confederate uniform. The rest of the men wore civilian clothes or a mixture of civilian with uniform—whatever they had been able to scratch up for themselves. This outfit didn't stand on ceremony.

Pulling his horse to a stop, one of the officers took a quick glance at the circled wagons. His face fell on Frio. "You had trouble?"

Frio pointed his chin south, toward the thinning dust left by the retreating Union troops. "We came almighty close to it. Yankees. They went yonder."

The officer said, "We'll catch them, don't you worry!" He shouted an order and spurred his horse. The company fell in behind him, shouting in a blood-thirsty eagerness. This would be their first contact with the enemy, if they could catch up. It would be a real horse race.

The Texas troops galloped away, their dust sweeping across the circled wagons and setting some of the teamsters to coughing. Happy Jack grinned. "If they overtake them Yankees, there'll sure be some whittlin' done."

The second body of riders trailed just a little way behind. Leading them was an officer in dust-gray uniform, sitting straight and proud in the saddle. He reined in at the wagons, his crow-tracked eyes sweeping the circle, taking in the defense preparations in one quick glance that told him all he really needed to know. Colonel Rip Ford asked, "Whose wagons?"

Frio stepped forward. "Mine, Colonel. Frio Wheeler."

The colonel stared, recognition coming into his eyes. He was a medium-tall man, this Rip Ford, with hair and short beard now mostly gray. He was still a year short of fifty, but the gray made him look older than he actually was, and some people with about as many years had grown accustomed to calling him "old" Rip Ford. Indeed, this man had lived more in those forty-nine years than many people could in ten lifetimes. Doctor, Ranger, legislator, trailblazer, newspaperman, soldier—he had been all of these things and still was. Often ignored by the higher-ups in government and military, made subordinate to men whose talents were far less than his own, Ford nevertheless had become something of a legend in his own lifetime among the people of Southern Texas. Some looked upon him almost as a latter-day Sam Houston. They believed Rip Ford could do anything he put his mind to, and they would remember him long after many of those who outranked him were forgotten.

"Frio Wheeler," Ford said in a quiet voice, beginning to smile. He extended his hand. "With all this dust in my eyes, and those whiskers on your face. . . ."

He came out of the saddle with a slow, stiff motion, for the ride had been long, and he was plainly weary. "Yankees try to take you?"

"They told us to give up our guns and our wagons. I never had a chance to answer them. They saw your dust and hightailed it south."

Still smiling, Ford said, "What was your answer going to be, or do I need to ask?"

The good nature of the officer eased Frio's coiled tension. "I was fixin' to say we wouldn't give up our guns, but they were welcome to what was in them."

Happy Jack had been eyeing the colonel with a youthful awe. He spoke up confidently, "We could've whipped twice as many, Colonel, and never broke a sweat."

Ford slumped wearily upon a wagon tongue and glanced southward. "We'll have to go in a minute. If

Captain Adams catches up and engages them, he'll need help." He peered at Frio with strong interest. "I've kept up with you, Frio Wheeler. I wish I had you in my command. But you're doing us more good where you are than you could in a uniform."

"I'd be right proud if I could ride with you, Colonel. I'd sure like to be there when you go back into Brownsville."

"Maybe that won't be long, Frio. I'm going to nibble at the fringes first, giving Herron trouble at his outposts, cutting off his patrols. I'll scatter my forces so he'll never know whether I have six hundred men or six thousand. I'll grind him down until he'll be glad to shake the dust of Brownsville from his feet."

Frio said again, "I'd like to be there when that happens."

The colonel stood up, bone tired and hating to leave. "Maybe you can, Frio. Maybe you can." He remounted his horse. "Good luck. And keep the wagons moving."

The teamsters waved their sombreros and cheered while Ford's long column passed by, moving into a lope, setting the choking dust aswirl. A warm elation rose in Frio. These men of Ford's were the hope of Southern Texas. Not a praying man, Frio nonetheless lowered his head and whispered, hoping God would hear.

Out in the edge of the chaparral, grim eyes observed from beneath a broad black sombrero. They had seen the whole thing—the Union approach and retreat. They had widened with surprised interest as Tom McCasland rode free and disappeared into the west. Now they watched in hatred as Frio Wheeler led his wagons once more out upon the trail.

The man wore a black neckerchief over his face. He

had allowed it to slip a little. Before turning back into the mesquite where a couple of his men waited, Florencio Chapa pulled the dusty neckerchief back up to cover all but his eyes. No one must ever see his face again. No one, perhaps, but Frio Wheeler. And that would be the last thing Wheeler ever saw on this earth!

15

RIP FORD WAS TIGHTENING the noose. Beneath a hot summer sun, his scattered men slowly approached the city of Brownsville from the north and the west. Not once since he had ridden down in April had all his troops ever come together at one time. Not once had Union intelligence been able to get even a fair approximation of Ford's strength. It seemed that everywhere the Union general Herron turned, the Texans were waiting for him. Herron had withdrawn his outposts one by one under Ford's unrelenting pressure, until now he had only Brownsville, and the thirty miles that stretched eastward toward the sea. He had five thousand federal troops at Fort Brown, or deployed eastward along the narrow-gauge railroad he had been building to carry supplies upriver from Brazos Santiago. For all Herron knew, Ford had that many men or more out in the dense *bosques*, awaiting only the order to move in and kill.

Now, so sick with fever that they had to help him into the saddle, Rip Ford stood his horse on the edge of one of the dried old riverbed *resacas*. Overhead, tall palm trees arched in the wind, their cupped fronds appearing almost black against the sky. Before him lay a scattering of Mexican *jacales*. Beyond these, in shimmering summer heat, stood a town waiting for deliverance.

"Brownsville." Ford tested the word fondly on his tongue and turned to Frio Wheeler, who sat on a sorrel horse beside him. "How long since you've seen it from the Texas side, Frio?"

"Been close to nine months now, Colonel."

"Perhaps it won't be long until you can ride down its streets again." Ford's voice was weak. His face was flushed and drawn from the siege of fever. But he had refused to allow anyone else to take over his command. For months now he had been preparing for the recapture of Brownsville. He had no intention of being on his back when the Texas troops moved into that town and raised their flag.

"Where do you suppose your wagons are, Frio?"

"I expect they ought to be at my ranch by now, sir. When we left San Antonio, folks were all excited about you whippin' the Yanks at Rancho Las Rucias. I figured that by the time my wagons got here, we could cross over at old Don Andres's ferry and save the miles we'd have to cover to Rio Grande City. With luck, I thought you might even have taken Brownsville."

"So you rode on ahead of the wagons to see how we fared?"

"Yes, sir. The wagons are in good hands. Happy

Jack Fleet, the young fellow you saw with me a while back, he was to take them to the ranch and wait."

Ford smiled thinly, and the smile was quickly gone. The colonel was suffering. "I appreciate your confidence. I only wish I *had* taken Brownsville already."

"You will, Colonel. It's like a ripe apple, ready to fall into your hands. And I want to have a part with you in the takin' of it."

Ford gazed with sadness at what he could see of the town. "It's been a good town to me, Frio. I've had some happy days there."

"Too bad you weren't in charge of Fort Brown when the Yankees first came. Things might've turned out different."

Ford shook his head. "Nobody could have stood off that many federals with the few troops the Confederacy had here. True, there are some things I'd've done differently. But the outcome would've been the same. Besides, *if* is the most futile word in the language. There ought to be a law against the use of it, at least in the past tense."

One of Ford's captains rode over and handed the colonel a long spyglass. "They've spotted us, sir. Yonder come some Union cavalry to give us a closer look."

Ford focused the instrument and held it a minute, scanning the dry landscape for sign of any other movement. He lowered the glass and nodded. "Good. There's a long *resaca* just ahead of them. As they move up out of it, tell the men to commence firing."

The captain argued, "Colonel, that's too long a range. We won't kill many Yankees thataway."

Ford shook his head. "I don't intend to. I never took pleasure in the death of any man, Captain, Yankee or what. If we can immobilize them or push them back without having to kill them, so much the better. There's been way too much killing in this war even as it is."

The colonel painfully started to swing out of the saddle. Frio and a couple of nearby officers were quick to step down and help him. Frio took the colonel's arm and could feel the heat of the fever, even through the sleeve. Ford thanked them when he was on his feet. An enlisted man in Mexican sombrero stood by to take the reins and hold the horse for him.

Ford said quietly to those around him: "Looking through the glass a few minutes ago, I saw the Union flag waving on its pole down at the fort. Gave me a bad feeling, really, knowing I was about to fire on it again. I always loved that flag." He glanced at Frio. "Did you know that during the time Texas was a republic I was in its Congress? Back in 1844, I was the man who introduced a resolution in the House proposing that Texas accept annexation into the United States." The sadness showed again in his face. "Ironic, isn't it? Now, after twenty years, I find myself fighting to keep Texas out of the United States."

He looked down, and Frio thought he could see tears in the colonel's eyes. Or maybe it was the fever. "There are some good men down there in that fort, beneath that flag. Some of them are friends of mine. It's a sad, sad thing to be forced to go to war against your friends."

He glanced up at Frio, and Frio nodded slowly.

The colonel added, "Any man can kill an enemy, if duty calls on him to do it. But it takes a strong man to be able to kill a friend."

A chill went through Frio.

The captain spoke up. "They've come to the riverbed, Colonel. Shall I give the boys the word to fire?"

Ford nodded regretfully. "Cut 'em loose."

Frio had his hands full just holding onto the sorrel horse when the firing started. The mount had not been around guns like most of the soldiers' horses had. The first volley was so deafening it brought a sharp pressure of pain against Frio's eardrums. Powder smoke began rising gray and thick from a couple of hundred positions along a scattered line. Through the drift of smoke, Frio could see a half dozen Union horses down. The Yankees had spread out suddenly but were still riding, coming head-on.

From this point the Texans spent no more volleys. There was a constant rattle of uneven fire as individual soldiers chose their targets and squeezed their triggers. The range was still long. Many of the bullets picked up dust from the parched ground in front of the federals. Now and again a horse would fall, or a man. The federals swept into another old riverbed. A few seconds later Frio expected to see them come up on this side, but they didn't. It occurred to him after a moment that they had taken cover in the bottom of the *resaca*, safe from the angry bullets of rebel guns. In a minute or two firing commenced over the rim of the old bed. The Union soldiers had dismounted and were answering fire with fire.

"A long-taw proposition," the captain said. "Neither side can do much like this."

Union bullets snarled harmlessly overhead, or dropped uselessly into the dust. Ford put up with it for a while. His men were firing only now and again as they saw a target. With them, ammunition was still too precious to waste. The federals were spending a lot more of it with no more results.

Presently Ford said, "Captain, let me see that glass again." He brought it to his eye and studied what part of the town was open to view. He nodded in satisfaction as he lowered the telescope. "It's about as I had expected. A Union relief column is on its way. Now is the time to give them a jolt." He pointed westward. "Is B Company deployed over yonder where I wanted them?" The captain nodded. "Yes, sir."

"Good," replied Ford. "If you-all will kindly help me onto my horse. . . ."

He swayed toward the mount. Frio and the others quickly went to his support. They helped him into the saddle. He looked down at Frio. "How about you, Frio? Want a closer look at Brownsville?"

Frio smiled. "Yep, Colonel, I sure do." He swung onto the sorrel.

To the captain, Ford said, "I'm going to take B Company and flank that *resaca*. I think when the Yanks see us coming they'll fog out of there in a hurry. As they do, you bring this company down. They'll be caught two ways. It's my hunch they'll stampede back toward the fort, and they'll carry that relief column with them."

The captain nodded, pleased. "I expect you'll spoil General Herron's supper, Colonel."

Ford replied, "Those Yankees have spoiled many a one of mine."

Too sick to be riding, but driven by his stern determination, Colonel Rip Ford led the way to where B Company waited in reserve. Frio had to spur to keep up with him. They reached the waiting men, who sat patiently smoking and telling yarns in the shadows of their horses.

The colonel said simply, "Boys, are you ready to go out there amongst them?" He turned his horse and started toward the *resaca*, trusting the men to follow after him. They did.

The range was still at least three hundred yards when the colonel said, "Into the skirmish line, boys, and let's hear you yell."

The men fanned out in a long, ragged line. At Ford's order, they moved into a gallop. The shrill yell started at the center and rippled up and down the line like a shock wave. It was a savage, exultant thing that made hair stand on the back of Frio's neck. He found himself swept along with it. He yelled too. Saddlegun in his hand, he stayed near the colonel. There was little target, for the federals were down in the safety of the old riverbed. But at Ford's order his men began firing anyway.

Moving up a rise, Frio saw alarm strike the dismounted Yankees with the force of a bombshell. They ran for their horses, swinging into their saddles. The officers were moving as fast as their men. Those who could not catch their horses, or who had lost them, swung up behind other men. The Yankees spurred over the rim of the riverbed. For a moment it looked as if they would retreat eastward. But over in that direction, another group of Ford's horsemen popped up as if by magic. And now the captain came from the center of the line with all his men.

The bluecoats had only one way to flee, and that was south. They ran headlong, maintaining no formation. Theirs was a panicked flight, every man for himself, for only God knew how many of those screeching Texans were pouring out of the brush behind them.

In pursuit, Ford's companies joined on the ends and made a solid line, moving forward at a gallop, sweeping down into the sandy old riverbeds and out again on the far side, dodging their horses around the palm trees. The Texans kept up a desultory fire that was aimed more at frightening than at a kill. It was hard to

shoot straight from the back of a running horse anyway. The man who claimed he could would probably
lie about other things too.

The fleeing federals overran the relief column without slowing down. For a moment the second group
of bluecoats seemed about to come forward and
give fight. But they changed their minds, turned their
horses about, and went running with the others, running for the cover they could find behind the lumber
and stone walls of the town. To Frio it was much like a
stampeding herd of cattle, sweeping up another herd in
its path.

Ford was falling behind, for in his condition he had
a hard time just staying in the saddle. He shouted for a
cease-fire and pullback, and somehow some of the
officers heard him through the din of hoofs and yelling
men and roaring guns. Gradually the Texans pulled
their horses to a stop almost within the edge of the
town itself. They obeyed the colonel's orders grudgingly, for they had gotten a small, sweet taste of victory, and it was hard now to spit out the apple.

Forming again at the point from which the charge
had begun, some of the officers voiced the same disapproval as their men.

Ford, who looked deathly tired now but nonetheless
pleased, simply shook his head and lowered himself
into the shade of a palm.

"You did fine, boys. Now we just let Herron stew
over this thing for a while. Then we'll see what
happens.

Night came, and Ford dispatched three men as spies
to enter the town. Wearing old Mexican clothes, they
could pass unnoticed wherever they wanted to go.
Much later the three came back. Frio could read vic-

tory in the square thrust of their shoulders, their broad grins as they approached the colonel's small fire.

"Colonel," one of them said cheerily, without a salute, "it's just like you figured. Herron's loadin' up and pullin' out. They say he's retreatin' down the river—givin' up the town for good."

The colonel nodded and stared a long time into the coals. At first Frio thought Ford was simply lost in thought. Then he saw the colonel's lips move ever so slightly, and he caught a fragment of a whispered prayer. At last Ford looked up, his fevered eyes proud as his gaze moved from one to another of the men who stood in the circle of firelight. "Well, boys, we've done it. We've put him on the run with a force not a quarter the size of his, and we've shed precious little blood in doing it."

An officer said with emotion, "Texas will never forget this day, Colonel."

Ford shook his head. "I'm afraid you're wrong; they *will* forget what we've done here today. But their forgetting it won't alter the fact that it was done. History doesn't change just because somebody fails to get credit."

He turned to Frio. "How would you like to be the first man to bring cotton wagons into Brownsville after the Union occupation?"

Frio felt a quick glow. "I'd be tickled, Colonel."

"Well, then you go on to that ranch of yours and fetch them. By the time you get back, I think you'll find Brownsville ready and waiting for you."

16

As a schoolboy, Frio had studied about the glory of ancient Rome, and his imagination had soared grandly as he had pictured the march of the victorious Roman legions along the Appian Way. These things came back to his mind now as he made his own much smaller and probably dustier triumphal entry into Brownsville at the head of a long line of cotton wagons.

It was just three months short of a year since the dark and terrible night Frio had ridden out of burning Brownsville, taking Amelia and Chico with him. On the surface, the town didn't seem to have changed much, except those sections that had been touched by the great fire. Some of the damaged buildings had been reconstructed. Others still lay as they had fallen, their charred shells like blackened skeletons, a scar upon the land.

Townspeople—Anglo and Mexican alike—stood in the street and cheered as the wagons rolled into view, the dust rising in a heavy fog behind them. Along Elizabeth Street, Frio could see Confederate and Texas flags flying from makeshift flagpoles and draped from second-story windows—flags wisely stored away these many long months of Union occupation.

Frio rode the sorrel horse that was his favorite. Amelia McCasland sat on the first wagon, face aglow as she entered the town that had so long been home. Chico rode on top of the cotton bales, waving with pride at the youngsters who watched him enviously. There was a touch of brag about him in the way he threw out his chest. This was the biggest day in the boy's life.

Rip Ford's Texas troops stood scattered up and down the street, being congratulated by the townsmen because they had made it possible for this wagon train to come into Brownsville. Other trains were bound to follow within days. All up and down the winding trails, riders were telling teamsters that Brownsville was open again, that they could cut south and quit the much longer routes that led to Laredo and Rio Grande City.

Two Mexican boys raced along afoot in front of the wagons, crying excitedly, *"Los algodones!"* The cotton men! Women waved handkerchiefs, and men shouted for joy.

Frio reined over and waited for the first wagon to pull up even with him so that he might ride beside Amelia. He wished they could have brought María along to see this show. But they had decided that the baby, born in April, was still too young to make the trip and breathe the thick dust of the wagon train. So

María had remained at the ranch with the infant son she had named Blas. Natividad de la Cruz was there, along with a pair of vaqueros, to watch out for her. A widower himself, Natividad had taken an increasingly protective attitude toward María. Someday, when her grief had faded and the proprieties had been observed, Natividad would present his own case.

Ahead of the wagon train was the site of the McCasland store. Frio watched Amelia closely, worried about her reaction when she would see whatever was left of the place. He needn't have worried. She looked, and a momentary sadness came into her eyes, but there were no tears. Someone had cleaned off the lot. All the charred lumber had been removed. Only the smoke-blackened foundation rocks remained.

Amelia spoke softly, "I guess Tom must have seen to it that the place was cleared. I'm glad he did."

It was the first time Frio had heard her speak her brother's name in months. Even when he had told her about Tom leading the Union patrol to try capturing the wagon train and about Frio's letting Tom escape into the brush, she had listened without a word of comment.

Frio said, "I expect Tom went back across the river when the Union troops left town."

Amelia nodded soberly. "He couldn't stay here."

They rode on down to the old cottonyard on the riverbank. As in other times, Hugh Plunkett stood there waiting, his face solemn but proud. He stepped to one side and waved the lead wagon on by. "Just take her down to the far end yonder," he yelled. He reached out with his big hand as Frio rode up. Frio leaned down to shake with him. "Just like it used to be, ain't it, Frio? Happy days have come again."

"Happy?" Frio said evenly. "Long as that infernal

war is still on, I don't expect there'll be any happy days." He looked out across the big, empty yard. "One thing isn't like it was. No cotton here."

"There'll be aplenty of it, though," Plunkett said. "Your train is just the start. Before long there'll be so much cotton here a man can't hardly count it all." He nodded briskly. "Yes, sir, we'll show them Yankees."

Frio saw a movement at Hugh Plunkett's little frame-shed, where the cotton agent kept his papers. A woman stood there. Plunkett turned to follow Frio's gaze.

Frio squinted. "That's Mrs. Valdez, isn't it?"

Plunkett nodded, his mouth turning down sadly. "She's been waitin' to see you, Frio. She's got somethin' to tell you." Hugh rubbed the back of his neck and looked away a moment. "Before you go talk to her, Frio, there's somethin' you ought to know. I ain't never told you because I promised her I wouldn't. But now I think you ought to know what you owe to her. She's the one came that night and told me the Yankees were goin' out to kill you. Wasn't for her, you'd be dead right now."

Frio and Amelia looked at each other in surprise. Frio reached up to help Amelia down from the wagon before it went all the way to the end of the yard for unloading. Chico clambered down by himself, jumping the large part of the way and springing nimbly to his feet after going down on hands and knees.

Hugh said, "Now you better go talk to Mrs. Valdez."

Luisa Valdez's face was tense, and her hands were clasped together across her breasts. Frio saw the corner of a white handkerchief between two of her fingers. She had been crying. He took off his hat. Amelia went directly to the woman and took her hands.

"Luisa," Amelia said, "you have no idea how much we owe you."

Luisa Valdez shook her head. "You owe me nothing." She dropped her chin. But Frio already had seen the tears in her dark eyes. She said, "This is a great day for you."

Frio replied, "But not for you, it seems. What's the matter, Mrs. Valdez?"

Head still down, she said tightly, "They sent me to tell you about Tom."

Frio frowned. "What about him? Who sent you?"

"Florencio Chapa. Or rather, his men. They have Tom. They say they will kill him unless . . ."

Amelia stiffened. "Unless what? What do they want?"

"They want for Señor Wheeler to go and set him free. Florencio Chapa says you owe him two thousand dollars. He says he will wait at the Gutierrez place, the muleyard at the edge of Matamoros. He has Tom there. He says if you do not bring him the money, he will kill Tom."

Frio clenched his fists. "What makes him think I would do anything to help Tom McCasland?"

"Chapa was in the chaparral the day you let Tom go before the Colonel Ford could capture him. Chapa says you are still Tom's friend. He says you will pay. He says you must come today and by yourself."

Amelia's face had gone white. She turned away, hands over her eyes. Watching her, Frio said, "I thought you didn't care anymore about what happened to Tom."

Amelia shook her head. "It's easy to say things in anger. But he's still my brother. Nothing has ever changed that."

Frio put his hands on her shoulders. "And you still love him."

"That doesn't ever stop. I wanted it to, but I couldn't help it. You can't go back on blood." She paused. "I never told you, Frio, because I didn't know how, and I've never let Natividad tell you. But while we were branding cattle for you, we were putting Tom's brand on some too."

Frio blinked in surprise. He looked back into the bleak face of Luisa Valdez. He said, "You saved my life."

Luisa Valdez slowly shook her head. "I will not ask you to save Tom's in return. I think Chapa cares little about the money. I think he only wants to get you there so he can kill you. Then perhaps he will kill Tom anyway. Chapa likes to see blood. It is like a sickness with him. So I do not ask you to go."

"But you're hopin' I will."

She didn't reply. She didn't have to, for he could see the answer in her face, in the way her hand gripped the tiny crucifix that hung from her neck.

Turning to Amelia, he said, "What do you want me to do?"

She threw her arms around him and buried her face against his chest. "I don't know, Frio. I just don't know."

The boy, Chico, stood nearby, frightened a little because the women were crying and he did not understand what was the matter.

Amelia cried, "Frio, I couldn't bear to lose you."

He stroked her hair. "If I stay here and do nothin', they'll kill Tom. So it comes down to kind of a contest, doesn't it? Which one is the most important, Tom or me?"

"Frio, how could I make a choice like that?"

"You don't have to. I'll go."

Her eyes were wide. "Chapa will try to kill you."

"I don't figure on makin' it easy for him."

"I'm not asking you to go, Frio. Don't go just for me."

Frio shook his head. "It's for all of you, I guess. You, because I love you. Mrs. Valdez, because I owe her my life. Tom because . . . because whatever he did, he thought he was right. Because for a long time he was my friend. And maybe because I keep rememberin' somethin' Rip Ford said to me. He said, 'Any man can kill an enemy, if duty calls on him to do it. But it takes a strong man to be able to kill a friend.' I guess Tom is a stronger man than I am. I had a chance to kill him, and I couldn't make myself do it."

He told Hugh Plunkett, Happy Jack, and the others what he was going to do. As expected, Happy put up an argument.

"You don't owe him nothin', Frio. If you ever did, you settled it that day you let him get away from Rip Ford."

Frio resolutely shook his head. "I'm goin'. I have to. And you men are all stayin' on this side of the river. I'm afraid if you try to interfere, they'll kill Tom."

"Chapa won't give you a chance!" Happy argued.

"He will if he wants that money."

Frio rode across on the ferry. It took him awhile at the British consulate to get the cash together. When he had it, he put it in a set of saddlebags and started upriver on the sorrel, toward the wagonyard. As always, he saw the washerwomen rinsing clothes in the Rio, though drought had caused the river to recede so much that they had to go far out into what was normally the riverbed to reach the water. Naked children splashed and played.

Riding, watching, Frio remembered with a tug of sadness the day he and Blas Talamantes had come this way together, headed for the Gutierrez place. Nervous now, Frio saw the brush corral of the Gutierrez wagon and muleyard ahead of him, and beyond that the portion of stone fence and the rock building.

Movement to his left brought him to a sudden stop. In an instant he had the saddlegun up and ready.

Happy Jack loped his horse out from between two brush *jacales*. Behind him lumbered a pair of the cotton wagons, both full of Frio's teamsters. The wagons bristled with guns.

Angrily Frio said, "Happy, what do you mean by this? I told you to stay on the other side of the river."

Happy was defiant. "So we disobeyed you. Fire us!"

Frio glared at them, but his anger couldn't hold. Gratitude swelled within him, despite his impatience. "Look," he said, "I know you want to help, and I wish you could. But Chapa said for me to come by myself. If you-all show up he's liable to panic and shoot Tom in cold blood."

Happy replied, "For all you know, he already has. And it's a cinch he aims to kill you too if he can. We want to see he don't get the chance."

Frio braced his hands on the saddle horn and leaned forward on stiff arms, letting his gaze roam across the eager Mexican *mulateros* who had come with Happy. He knew he might need their help. He wished he could figure a way to use them. But he said, "No, boys, you-all stay back out of the way. You're liable to be more of a liability than an asset."

Happy was plainly of a mind to argue, but finally he shrugged. "All right, Frio, play the game your way. But we'll be here. First sign of double cross, we'll be on top of Chapa like a hawk on a rabbit."

Frio nodded. "Thanks, Happy. Thanks to all of you. Now, you must let me handle it."

Riding ahead, he kept his eyes on the rock building.

There was no sign of life, and the wooden door was closed, but he could feel eyes watching him through the two open windows that faced to the front. A chill played up and down his back. He tightened his muscles, half expecting a bullet to knock him out of the saddle. His breath was short as he stopped the sorrel horse and stepped down carefully from the saddle. He unfastened the saddlebags and draped them across his left arm, holding the saddlegun in his right. Standing beside the stone fence, a hundred feet from the door, he called.

"Chapa! Chapa, you in there?"

He heard movement inside. He still had that chilling feeling that eyes were watching every move he made.

A voice answered from behind the rock wall. Frio thought he saw a man behind one of the windows. "Gringo, did you bring the money?"

Frio raised his left arm a little. "I brought it. Got it right here."

"Bring it."

Frio shook his head. "No. I came for Tom McCasland. You turn him loose out here and you get the money."

"Bring the money here and you will have your friend."

"And give you a chance to shoot me down at the door? No, I came to trade with you, not commit suicide."

"You have no choice. Bring the money."

"You just come on out here and get it."

Silence. Then a Spanish command was shouted out a side window. Chapa's voice said, "Gringo, you are a fool. I have men outside. They will take you *and* the money!"

Frio glanced to his right. Three men hurried toward

him from behind another building. At his left, he saw two men rise up from where they had crouched behind the brush fence.

Trapped! he thought, in sudden desperation.

Two shots barked. The Chapa men stopped abruptly. Happy Jack and the teamsters rushed out from their hiding place, guns ready. The Chapa men hesitated, knowing they were caught in the open, that they couldn't get away. They dropped their guns. At a command from Happy Jack, they walked out with their hands up.

Relief washed over Frio. If it hadn't been for Happy. . . .

He shouted at Chapa, "I have men too. They've come to see that you give me an honest deal. Now show me Tom McCasland."

"He is here. I do not lie to you."

"I don't believe you. I think you've already killed him. Before you get this money you've got to bring him out here and show me he's still alive."

There was a minute or two of quiet, as Chapa and those with him inside the building talked it over. Finally the door opened. Tom McCasland stepped out into sunlight, his hands tied behind him. With him came the renegade Bige Campsey. Frio narrowed his eyes. Tom was disheveled, and a big splotch of dried blood showed on the side of his head.

Campsey said loudly, "All right, Wheeler, here's your friend. Come get him and bring the money."

Frio stood undecided. He liked this rock fence in front of him for protection. Once he stepped beyond it, he was an easy target.

Campsey said, "Come on, Wheeler! We ain't goin' to wait all day!"

Frio felt his mouth go dry. He gripped the saddlegun

so tightly that his hands cramped. But he looked at Tom, and he decided there was no choice but to take the risk. He moved toward the open gate.

Tom saw what Frio was about to do. "No, Frio!" he shouted.

Campsey turned to strike Tom. Tom bumped his body against the renegade. Caught off balance, Campsey staggered. Tom ran toward Frio, moving awkwardly because his hands were bound at his back.

"It's a trap, Frio!" he shouted. "They're goin' to kill you!"

Campsey raised his pistol. Before Frio could bring the saddlegun into line, the pistol barked. Tom stumbled and went down. Frio's rifle blazed. Campsey was slammed back against the wooden door. He staggered two steps out from the building, trying to bring the pistol up again. Then he fell forward on his face and lay still.

Frio shouted, "Tom!" And started to go on out. Guns flamed from the windows. Bullets flattened against the stone fence, forcing Frio back. But he had time to see Tom lying on the ground, motionless.

From behind Frio came the sound of other guns. His men had seen Tom go down, and they figured there no longer was anything to lose, no reason to stand back. They came running, Happy Jack out in front. They fired as they ran. At least twenty men joined Frio at the rock fence. Others circled around to the sides. They poured a murderous fire into, or at, the open windows. Powder smoke clung thick and choking. Inside that stone building the ricochets must be pure hell.

Happy Jack said triumphantly to Frio, "See there, I told you Chapa wouldn't tote fair. He's got no respect for an owner."

Frio raised his hand. The gunfire eased off. He took

a long look across the fence. Tom had crawled a few feet, but now he lay still again.

"Chapa," Frio called, "you haven't got a chance anymore. Come on out of there with your hands up."

He heard angry argument from inside the building. The door opened. Half a dozen *bandidos* came out with hands over their heads. Some of them bled from wounds inflicted by the ricochets. A fat man crawled on his hands and knees, sobbing in terror, begging for mercy. This was El Gordo Gutierrez.

Frio waited, but there was no sign of the man he wanted.

"Chapa! No use you stayin' in there. Come on out!"

A voice cursed in violent Spanish, and a gun flashed in a window. A slug whined off the rock fence, sending stone chips flying.

"Gringo!" Chapa shouted. "Do you hear me?"

"I hear you."

"Your friend, he still lives. But I can kill him from here."

Dismayed, Frio realized the outlaw was right. Frio could see that Tom was breathing. He knew the *bandido* could fire on Tom from the darkness behind the window or the open door.

"If you kill him, you'll never get out of there alive!" Frio answered.

"Every man has to die sometime. He likes to take his enemies with him."

Frio swallowed, knowing he was helpless. It was hard to get any leverage against a man who was unafraid of death. "All right, Chapa, what do you want?"

"I want you, gringo! We finish this fight, the two of us. Nobody else."

Dread crept over Frio. He looked around him, desperately clutching for some idea. But none came.

Tom would die for certain if Frio didn't act. "All right, Chapa. We both step out into the open. It'll be just us two, no more."

"Agreed. Come ahead."

Frio moved toward the open gate. Happy Jack stepped forward as if to stop him. Resolutely, Frio shook his head. "I'm goin' to do it, Happy. Chapa and me, we've had this a-buildin' for a long time. Stay out of it."

He walked into the open, the saddlegun in his right hand, hanging free at his side. He saw a movement inside the building and steeled himself, half expecting treachery. But Chapa was true to his word. He appeared in the doorway. For just a moment the bandit's eyes touched the dead Bige Campsey. Then they lifted back to Frio.

Chapa's face was covered by a black neckerchief, all but his eyes. He stood one pace out from the door, those evil eyes narrowed with hatred. Dry-lipped, Frio moved toward him slowly, watching for the first indication of movement. Chapa gripped a pistol in his left hand, his arm hanging at his side. The right hand, which should have held the pistol, was shriveled and misshapen, like a claw. It was useless. Frio realized this must have happened to Chapa the night the pistol had exploded in his hand, near his face. That was the reason for the mask. The face must have suffered like the hand did.

Frio kept walking, closing the distance between the two of them. He was aware that Tom had raised himself up on one elbow. Tom was calling weakly for him not to go through with this. But Frio went on.

Chapa said in a raw, lashing Spanish, "You have come far enough, gringo. Before you die, I want you to see what you have done to me."

Black eyes burning, Chapa slowly raised the claw-like hand to the mask over his face. Frio swallowed, not wanting to see, but he was held by some strange compulsion.

The hand ripped the neckerchief away. Frio gasped aloud, not ready for the hideous thing that had been a face. "Look, gringo," Chapa hissed, "see what you have done to me! See why I am going to kill you!" The face was a mass of angry red scar tissue from the cruel burn of the powder. The nose was half gone. The vicious mouth had healed back crookedly after white-hot metal had torn the lips.

Chapa said, "It makes your stomach sick, *verdad*? Think of how it must feel to own such a face and have to hide it behind a mask because children scream at the sight of it, and women turn away. For months I have wanted to die. But even more, I have wanted you to die. I have told myself that if I could see you dead, I would walk into the fires of hell content."

Chapa's eyes smoldered with the hatred that had eaten at him like a cancer. "My left hand is slow with the pistol. I know you will kill me, and I am ready. But before I die, I will also kill *you*. We will go to hell together."

Frio saw the *bandido*'s hand start up with the pistol. "Die, gringo!" Instantly Frio dropped to one knee, swinging the saddlegun around. Without waiting to raise the stock to his shoulder, he squeezed the trigger. The rifle leaped.

Chapa stepped back under the impact. The pistol blazed. The bullet snarled over Frio's head. Chapa buckled, bending forward from the waist. His eyes were on Frio to the last. He tried with all the ebbing strength that was in him to raise the pistol again. He never could.

"Gringo!" he hissed. "Gringo *apeztoso!*"

Even after death came, Chapa lay there on one shoulder, his glazed eyes still open, his pitifully butchered face scowling the bitter hatred that he had carried into death.

Tom McCasland lay pale and still in his little Matamoros house. Luisa Valdez sat in a chair at the head of the bed, silently watching him, a glow of contentment about her. Tom was hit low in the shoulder. The doctor had said he would live, though he might be months in recovering. Those were months in which he wouldn't be riding out—months during which she would not be spending the dark, lonely nights wondering if he would come back alive. For these months, at least, she would have him.

Frio Wheeler stood frowning down at Tom. "One thing you can say about that Bige Campsey, he was a consistent shot. He hit you in the same place he hit me."

Lying on his side, Tom looked up at Frio. "I never expected you to come help me. You didn't owe me anything. Why did you do it?"

Frio looked first at Luisa, then at Amelia, who stood beside him, her hand on his arm. "The women, for one thing. And, I reckon, for us. We were friends a long time before we were enemies, Tom. When it came right down to the taw line, I couldn't forget that."

Tom said gravely, "You know that as soon as I can get up from here and ride again, I'll be fightin' you the same as before."

Frio nodded, his face sober. "I know. I'll likely be fightin' you too. We've each fought this war accordin' to our own lights and done all we could for the side we were loyal to. Whichever way it goes, we've given our best. We've got nothin' to be ashamed of, either of us. Maybe someday, when the war is finished, we can find a way to be friends again."

Tom said, "It's liable to be hard. There's been a lot come between us."

"But it'll be worth the tryin'. Even if the South wins, nobody believes the country can stay divided. We'll have to find a way to stop bein' enemies and be friends again. The North and the South—you and me. It had just as well start with you and me."

Tom said, "I'd like to try."

Frio nodded. "We'll do it, Tom. Now Amelia and me, we're goin' back to the other side of the river. It's where we belong now. Get yourself plenty of rest." He glanced at Luisa. "I know you won't lack for good care."

Amelia bent and kissed Tom on the cheek. "We'll see you again, Tom, when this thing is over."

Frio was at the door when Tom called him. "Frio, you goin' to marry my sister?"

Frio nodded again, and a faint smile came to his face. "Never was any doubt about it."

Arm in arm, Frio Wheeler and Amelia walked down the dusty street of Matamoros toward the river. Ahead of them, far across on the Texas side of the Rio Grande, the Stars and Bars of the Confederacy caught the wind and billowed out atop the tall flagpole in Fort Brown. How long it was destined to stay there, no man could say. All Frio knew for certain was that for however long it lasted, it was a proud sight to see. . . .

And in the end. . . .

The last battle of the Civil War was fought at Palmito Hill, some twelve miles downriver from Brownsville, May 13, 1865.

After retreating from Brownsville, the federal forces had taken an ineffective holding position at Brazos Santiago, where they then remained through the rest of the war. Some of the Union officers plotted quietly with the Mexican border chieftain Cortina, whose political position had been made precarious by French imperialist victories over the poorly armed patriots of Benito Juarez. Cortina was to capture Brownsville with his own troops in return for a commission as a brigadier general in the United States Army. The stand-firm leadership of Colonel Rip Ford brought these plans to naught.

Finally, in March, the Texan and Union forces signed a truce, agreeing that further bloodshed along the Rio Grande would serve no useful purpose in the far larger war rapidly reaching its climax in the Deep South.

When news came early in May of General Lee's surrender at Appomattox, about two thousand bales of Confederate cotton remained on the riverbank in Brownsville. Northern cotton speculators in Matamoros, eager to get their hands on the cotton, persuaded the Union general that he should proceed to take it in the name of the Union even though such a move would violate the truce.

Under Colonel T. H. Barrett, sixteen hundred Union troops moved upriver toward Brownsville. News of Lee's surrender had thinned Rip Ford's Texas forces, but he was still able to muster about three hundred men, including the intrepid Benavides. He marched downriver and met the federals at Palmito Hill. Incredibly, his three hundred determined riders not only defeated the Union force but actually chased it seven miles before Ford called a halt.

"Boys," said that gallant man, "we have done finely. We will let well enough alone and retire."

This was his quiet benediction to four tragic, needless years of conflict.

It was ironic that even though the Confederacy already had lost the war, it won its final battle in a futile blaze of glory on a desolate, sandy stretch of coastal wasteland fifteen hundred miles from Richmond.

Westerns available from

TRAPPER'S MOON • Jory Sherman

"Jory Sherman takes us on an exhilarating journey of discovery with a colorful group of trappers and Indians. It is quite a ride."—Elmer Kelton

THE PUMPKIN ROLLERS • Elmer Kelton

When Trey McLean leaves his family's cotton farm and sets off on his own, he's about as green as they come. But Trey learns fast—about deceit and love when he meets the woman he's destined to marry.

CASHBOX • Richard S. Wheeler

"A vivid portrait of the life and death of a frontier town."—*Kirkus Reviews*

SHORTGRASS SONG • Mike Blakely

"*Shortgrass Song* leaves me a bit stunned by its epic scope and the power of the writing. Excellent!"—Elmer Kelton

CITY OF WIDOWS • Loren Estleman

"Prose as picturesque as the painted desert..."—*The New York Times*

BIG HORN LEGACY • W. Michael Gear

Abriel Catton receives the last will and testament of his father, Web, and must reassemble his family to search for his father's legacy, all the while pursued by the murdering Braxton Bragg and desire for revenge and gold.

Available by mail from

TOR
FORGE

DEATHRIGHT • Dev Stryker

"Two bestselling authors combine forces to write a fast-paced and exciting terrorist thriller. Readers will want to stay the course."—*Booklist*

RED CARD • Richard Hoyt

"A brave smart shot...heaps of soccer lore....Hoyt manages to educate as he entertains."—*Publishers Weekly*

DEAD OF WINTER • David Poyer

A thrilling novel of revenge by the bestselling author of *The Only Thing to Fear.*

FALSE PROMISES • Ralph Arnote

"Guaranteed to please all fans of non-stop, cliffhanger suspense novels!"
—*Mystery Scene*

CUTTING HOURS • Julia Grice

"Readers will find this hard to put down. Love, hate, and a mother's determination to save her daughter make for a ten

WINNER TAKE ALL • Sean Flannery

"Flannery is a major find."—Dean Koontz

ULTIMATUM • R.J. Pineiro

"The purest thriller I've seen in years. This book may define the genre."
—Stephen Coonts

OTTO'S BOY • Walter Wager

"New York City's subway becomes a deathtrap in Wager's taut thriller."—*Library Journal*